GRAHAM

THE BROTHERS OF HASTINGS RANCH SERIES
BOOK ONE

By Katharine E. Hamilton

ISBN-13: 978-0-578-67482-7

Graham

www.katharinehamilton.com

Cover Design by Kerry Prater.

To my husband, Brad.
A true steward of the land and an awesome hubs.
In the words of our son, Everett, "Daddy is a good dad, a good Brad, and he's my best friend."
I agree.

Acknowledgments

It would have been nice to just take some snapshots of my cowboy husband and, wa la, have a cover for the book. But alas, that is not how it works. Plus, my husband would not agree to it. Yes... I asked. Ha! So, thanks to my cover designer, Kerry Prater, for helping me search for the perfect picture of Graham and for designing such an awesome cover.

Thank you to my editor, Lauren Hanson. Both of us are expecting babies soon, so to say this project required a lot of effort is an understatement. Through morning sickness, Covid-19, and just the usual pregnancy woes, we seemed to get it done. Thanks, Lauren!

My husband, Brad, whom NONE of the characters are based on. (Wink wink.) After 7 years of marriage and ranch living, there was much educating me on his part to help me write several scenes. But I sure did, and do, enjoy the rides around the ranch with my handsome cowboy. And his heart to be a steward of the land and to God's creatures is a true calling. And though it has been 7 years of ranch life for me, I still have MUCH to learn and he's a great teacher.

Taehlor Gordon, horse lover and expert, for being my horse educator and answering some of my horse questions... of which I will have many more.

H

Chapter One

She'd been driving for days. At least, that's what it felt like. She still wasn't quite sure why Alice requested her to pick up so much food, or why her friend asked her to drive to the middle of God-forsaken nowhere. But Alice never was one to give details. About anything. Work. Life. Men. She kept it simple and to the point. No fluff. And that was one of the attributes Julia loved about her. And one of the reasons Julia was driving all the way from Santa Fe, New Mexico to some podunk west Texas town to stay for a few weeks. She hadn't taken a vacation in years. It wasn't a hardship, really, to be dedicated to her work. She loved working at the museum in downtown Santa Fe. The Palace of the Governors was a top tourist destination before travelers ventured to see the rest of the city. And Julia McComas was Santa Fe born and raised. There was no better person for the job of educating newcomers to the artsy city.

But when a friend called in need of some serious girl time, you left work, took that overdue vacation time, and went. Again, no details from Alice as to why she sounded so desperate on the phone for Julia to make the trip, but her old college roommate didn't need to ask twice. In fact, she didn't need to ask at all. Julia could tell by the tone of Alice's voice that she was overwhelmed and frantic about something. It also took something huge for Alice Wilkinson to request a visit, so Julia didn't hesitate. She packed her bags and headed towards the town of Parks, Texas.

Parks. Even the name of the town was bland, but she tried to remain upbeat. She'd stopped in the last town and picked up food from a local restaurant which boasted vegan specialties that even had her carnivore heart salivating at the mouth. She'd attempted a small chain barbecue joint, but the filth on the door and the ragged parking lot deterred her and she found a nice hole in the wall café that seemed extremely out of place for the small town. But Alice had said that Parks only had one diner, and that any hope for multiple options on food would need to be found in Sheffield. So that's what Julia had done. Though again, the sheer amount of food she'd had to purchase from the place had left a dent in her wallet. But the avocado and toasted tempeh sandwiches along with the ranch chickpea sandwiches and the delicious sounding menu she'd perused, had her ordering one of each sandwich, stuffing them in a cooler that she had to purchase as well, and heading the last few miles towards Parks.

She was expected to meet Alice at a ranch outside of town. The Hastings Ranch. Her friend was on site for the day and hoped to be breaking for lunch about the time Julia arrived. So far, Julia had passed a dirt road, a gravel road, a weird looking shrub, and a dead animal carcass. *All promising signs*, she thought. Nothing that pointed her to the elusive ranch. When she'd almost given up hope, a sign for Parks, population: 1,088, welcomed her into the city limits.

A gas station, tire shop, feed store, parts store, and what looked to be a small post office made up the main street. She spotted a tattered building the next block over and realized that was the fine dining establishment Alice had mentioned. She shuddered and kept driving. Lord have mercy on her soul if she had to step foot in that place during her stay. She followed the road out of downtown and immediately fell back into the groove of driving through no-man's land. "Twenty miles outside of town" is what Alice had told her. "On the right."

She assumed there'd be signage of some sort, but so far, zilch. Nada. Nothing that assured her she was headed in the right direction. She spotted tall wooden posts up ahead on the right and slowed her speed. A large metal 7H hung from a cedar beamed entry. Was this the place? She wasn't sure, but at this point, she'd take the risk and see. She could always ask for directions if she was in the wrong place. Turning onto the gravel and dirt-patched road, she cringed when her tire hit a hole the size of Texas and gripped her steering wheel with a bit more force. Dust billowed behind her as she seemed to be driving blindly into yet another empty space. Ten minutes later, hope kindled, as she spotted trucks, cows, machinery, pens, and what looked like people up ahead. She sighed in relief as she saw the "Sheffield Veterinary Clinic" logo on the side of a white truck and realized she'd found the correct place. Alice was the local vet. Her office was in Sheffield, "the city," though she covered Parks and surrounding areas. She turned off the engine and opened the door, her wedge heel crunching rock and dirt beneath her foot. Annoyed that she'd have to wipe her shoes down later, she mustered a smile as she closed the door and looked for Alice.

Cows bellowed as their baby calves were separated from them amongst metal pens that seemed to be radiating the sun's deathly rays. Heat and stench rushed over her as she stepped around a mud-stained truck closer to the action. Yells and slaps could be heard as she finally spotted her friend inside the pen with the calves. She watched as Alice pulled what looked to be a poker stick from a flame and pushed it into the hide of one of the calves. The sizzling sound and the squelch from the calf would haunt Julia later, she knew, along with the terrible smell... make that *smells*... that seemed to perfume the air. She held her hand over her mouth and nose as she waved to get attention. Anyone's attention. The calf hopped away from Alice and within seconds was perfectly content, despite the branding. She watched as another calf was fed through a slim shaft towards three men standing at the other end, Alice penciling something on a clipboard as the calf was held and flipped by metal bars to its side. She watched as one man, a cowboy hat slung low over his face, issued some sort of medical treatment into the calf's mouth and pierced its ear with a tag. While two other men— She gasped as she watched in horror. One man stood, holding the back leg of the calf outward while the other man— She couldn't watch. It was too much. Yet she couldn't look away as she watched the man castrate the animal without batting an eye. The animal was flipped back to its feet, released from the chute and sent outward, where it received a poke from Alice's flaming rod before scurrying out into the pen at the other end. Julia stood in shock and disgust. Had she seriously just witnessed what she thought she'd witnessed? And Alice just stood by and wrote something on her clipboard, no care in the world, as if this were a normal practice. Perhaps it was. Julia didn't know. But it was a sight she'd never forget. And before she could catch her breath, the men were doing it all over again. She waved her hand when Alice turned and offered a

"Yoohoo!" But her friend didn't see her. She spotted a gate to the pen where the cows, she was sure, watched in agony over their babies as they underwent the necessary treatments. She figured she could sidestep the mammals and reach Alice safely to let her know of her arrival.

Slipping into the pen, she stepped over a pile of fresh manure with a grimace. Spotting a cow before her, she smiled and held both her hands up in peace, her new turquoise bracelet sliding down her forearm, as she slowly shuffled around the beast, making sure to give it a wide berth. She'd successfully wound her way to the nearest corner of the pen that placed her near the work area. She cleared her throat, but still could not be heard over the calves, cows, and men all vying to talk over one another. Frustrated, she placed her hands on her hips and began to step towards the group when she heard a deep bellowing moo behind her and felt the speckle of saliva that sprinkled over her arm. She jumped and took a quick step back as an angry cow glowered at her.

"Easy girl. Easy." Julia held her palms out and hopped back another step, as her peace treaty stance only seemed to anger the cow more. One of the back hooves lifted and kicked dirt behind her, a clear sign of irritation from any species. Julia glanced towards the workers and estimated the number of strides it would take for her to spring their direction and whether or not she could beat an oncoming cow. She was quick. She ran every day. Not in wedged heels, but she could manage it if she needed to. Women ran in heels all the time... in movies. Panicked at the vengeful snort sent her direction and the speed in which the cow charged, Julia braced herself for impact. Screaming, she closed her eyes and felt her back slam into the fence, only it wasn't a cow that pinned her back against the pens, but a sweaty-faced man who'd expertly saved her from a charging mass of bovine maternal instinct. Her heart raced as she watched another man tame the cow and nudge it back into the midst of its surrounding companions. Relieved and grateful for the man's rescue, Julia started to speak, but her words were cut off by an incoherent stream of insults as a tall man nearest the latest entrapped calf stepped back, holding his bloody hand up for everyone's perusal.

∞

"You idiot!" Graham screamed. His eyes, somewhat hidden beneath his cowboy hat, seethed as he stomped towards his younger brother. Grabbing the front of Seth's shirt, he slammed him into the pens. Seth's eyes widened as he spotted Graham's injured hand and the temper that would end with a punch in the gut or nose. "What were you thinkin'?" He released Seth's shirt as he took a step back and allowed Alice to grab his hand. His brother had abandoned his post on the calf, releasing the back leg just as Graham was slicing to castrate, the calf kicking out and causing him to slice the knife through himself instead. His eyes landed on the terrified woman just a few short steps away from Seth. "Who are you? And what in the—" He took a deep breath to control his anger, but to no avail. "What are you doing in my pens?"

Alice looked up then. "Julia?"

Julia gave a sheepish wave. "I'm here."

Graham fired a look at Alice.

"She's my friend. I asked her to come," Alice explained as she wrapped a torn bandana around his hand.

"Here? Now?" Graham shook his head in disgust. "You," He pointed to Seth. "get back to your post. Hayes!" he screamed, and another brother in the back pen looked up. Graham held up the blood-soaked hand and without a word, Hayes swung his legs over the fence and hurried over. "What happened?"

"Ask the nit-wit." Graham nodded towards Seth. "Make sure he doesn't leave his post again. Finish up."

Hayes nodded, without even a single glance in Julia's direction, before heading towards Graham's position at the calf chute. Seth fumbled an apology to Graham and Graham gave him an extra helpful shove in the direction of the calf chute that had the younger brother tripping over his boots a couple of steps before righting himself and refocusing on his task.

"Get this cleaned up," Graham told Alice, nodding towards his hand. "Hayes doesn't need to cover me for long or we'll have a mess on our hands."

"Calm down." Alice, annoyed, pulled back the bandana. She saw Julia's face blanch. "Come to my truck. We've got to clean it."

Graham stormed through the center of the pen, the cows parting for him as though he were Moses crossing the Red Sea.

"What were you doing coming into the pens?" Alice asked Julia as they followed behind him.

"I waved and yelled but you didn't hear me. I was just going to sneak around to hearing distance and let you know I'd arrived. I didn't expect a mean cow to go crazy at me. Thankfully that guy saved me."

"Seth," Alice told her. "He did, and I'm glad, but he also injured his brother in the process. Graham is not going to be happy."

"I can tell that already. I didn't mean for this to happen," Julia whispered.

Graham plopped down on the bed of Alice's truck, his hand in his lap and watched as his friend walked slowly with the woman that interrupted their work. *Foolishly* interrupted their work. Heels, short shorts, frilly top... the woman was definitely not from around Parks.

"How we doin', Graham?" Alice asked, as she fished her vet bag out of the main cab of her truck and walked towards him.

"How does it look like I'm doin'?" he growled. "'Bout sliced my hand off because of Thing One and Thing Two." He nodded towards Julia and then in Seth's direction.

Alice glanced at his cut again. "You're going to need stitches."

"Just super glue it. It'll be fine."

"No, this one needs actual stitches. You sliced yourself pretty bad. It's deep. Glad it wasn't a little higher; you could have hit some nerves."

"Oh, my nerves were hit," he confirmed. "Just not in my hand."

Alice snickered. "Easy now. Don't be annoyed at the newbie. She didn't realize her appearance would spook the cows."

"Who walks up on working calves and thinks it's a good idea to go traipsing through the cow pen?" He flipped his hat off his head and swiped his arm over his forehead before slamming the straw hat back onto his head.

"I am truly sorry about that." Julia stepped forward, her eyes flashing towards his hand and then back to his face. "I didn't know how else to—"

"Right. You didn't know. Yet you walk into a working ranch in the middle of an operation like you own the place, pissing off a cow *and* me, 'bout get me to cut off my own hand, and you think I want to hear 'I'm sorry'?"

"Graham." Alice's tone warned him to dial his frustration back a notch, but nothing made him madder than someone completely irresponsible in the midst of cattle work.

"Couldn't wait ten minutes?" Graham barked. "We had five calves left. Five!"

"Again, so sorry." Julia's apology sounded shaky as he noted the glassy eyes and flamed cheeks. He didn't care for tears, especially a woman's tears. And to his disappointment, his anger faded a few degrees.

"Don't pay him any mind, Julia," Alice said, as she poured straight alcohol over his wound with a satisfied grin. Graham fought back the urge to jump up and howl in pain, and just bit down his complaints on a groan. "Graham's always sour. Why don't you fetch me the small white box in my bag?" She nodded towards the black leather bag sitting next to Graham. Julia cautiously approached the truck bed, and clumsily clutched the box and handed it to Alice. "Hold still, Graham."

"I am."

"No, you're not. You're about to shoot off this truck and strangle Julia. And then Seth. And then anyone else who gets in the way. Sit still."

Graham didn't even look at the other woman, even though she was nice to look at. It wasn't every day they had a pretty woman turn up on the ranch, but her stupidity had him questioning her intelligence, and that helped deter any reaction to her presence other than tolerance. *Minimal* tolerance. He watched as Alice quickly stitched through his skin and closed the gaping slice with an expert seam. She clipped the end of the string. "There. See? As good as new."

"Still hurts like—"

"I know," Alice finished. "Take some pain relievers. Keep an eye on it for infection. You should be fine."

"Fit as a fiddle." Hayes's voice drifted over to them. "All calves complete. They're in the trap waiting to be matched up with their mommas. Figure we'll release them tomorrow?"

Graham nodded, annoyed that work had to be pushed to the next day because of his hand. "That's fine. Clean up. I'll match 'em up. We're done here for today. Lunch time's 'bout here anyway."

"Lunch time was two hours ago," Alice quipped and then playfully punched his arm as she bagged up her supplies. "But, lucky you, I had Julia bring back some barbeque sandwiches from Sheffield." She eyed Julia in hope and her face sank at what she saw. "You remembered, right?"

Julia nodded begrudgingly, but then she gave an excited smile. "I brought lunch..." She hesitated. "But not barbecue."

"Oh?" Alice's brow rose.

"Have you seen that place?" Julia asked. "The parking lot is made of shredded rubber tires."

"And?" Graham asked.

The woman's brown eyes widened as her turquoise earrings dangled. "And that's disgusting. And the door was a screen door. Barely on the hinges."

"It's an old building," Graham defended. "Everyone knows the best barbecue is in Sheffield."

"Well, I found someplace better." Julia turned on her heel and stalked towards her car, her ankles wobbling on the unstable ground due to her heels.

"She *would* drive a sporty little death trap," Graham mumbled.

"Be nice," Alice whispered back. "She's not from around here."

"No kidding?" Sarcastically, he looked down at Alice and her narrowed gaze told him she was seriously thinking about beating him up already. "What's she doing here, Alice?"

"She's going to stay with me a few weeks."

"Why? Runnin' from somethin'?"

"No."

"That type of woman... coming to Parks. She's definitely runnin' from somethin'. Why else would she come here?"

"Because I asked her to." Alice's annoyed tone had him glancing down at her.

"I see."

"Don't 'I see', me." Alice pointed her finger up at him. "Be nice for once. She's doing me a favor."

"Gates are all secure." Clint, another Hastings brother walked up, slapping his hat on his leg to shake the dust out, and then plopped it back onto his sweaty hair. "Lawrence took the horses back to the barn. Said he'd be up here after. I'm starving. Where's lunch?" He looked to Alice and she nodded towards Julia leaning halfway into her back seat to retrieve a large red cooler. Clint grinned and accepted the slap to the chest Alice gave him for checking out her friend. "I do believe I need to be a gentleman." He hurried towards Julia's car and flashed his devilishly handsome smile, hat in hand, as he offered to carry the cooler towards the back of Alice's truck. When he opened the lid, his smile fell. "What is this?"

Julia beamed as she reached into the cooler. "There was this charming little sandwich shop in Sheffield, sort of off the beaten path. Their menu was to die for, so I ordered one of everything. Here." She handed him a deli wrapped sandwich.

He opened it, and his brow furrowed as he thumbed the bread down with dirty fingers to look inside the edge. "Where's the meat?"

Julia continued smiling and gave an encouraging nod. "It's vegan."

Graham's snort had Julia nervously glancing his direction.

"But just as filling," she continued. "That one is roasted chickpeas. Great protein," she recited to Clint. "And *you* can have..." She fished around inside the cooler and pulled another sandwich out. "This one." She handed it to Graham.

He unwrapped it. "Avocado?"

She nodded.

He tossed the sandwich onto the bed of the truck. "If I wanted mushy avocado, I'd make myself some guacamole." He stormed off towards his truck. "I'll be at the house, eatin' a *real* sandwich." Slamming his door, he made sure to cast one last disapproving glare towards Alice's friend. "Avocado," he muttered in disbelief. "Over my dead body."

—H—

Chapter Two

"Well, that didn't go well." Julia closed the lid to the cooler as the group of weary, hungry cowboys dragged their feet towards their trucks.

"They all ate. That's the important thing." Alice closed her tailgate and smirked as she studied Julia watching the Hastings brothers walk away. "Not a bad picture, is it?"

"Hm?" Julia turned and then rolled her eyes. "Please. They're covered in dirt, sweat, and cow manure, and I'm pretty sure half of them haven't seen a shower and a shave in months."

Alice shrugged. "Hard work requires a little dirt. Why don't you follow me up towards the house? I want to make sure Graham took something for his hand."

"I don't think I need to be anywhere near that man. He'd probably kill me."

"Yeah. Probably. But won't that be fun?" Alice chuckled as she hopped into her truck and gunned the engine with the full expectation that Julia would follow along behind her.

They didn't have to drive far. A few miles down the gravel road sat a large, wood-framed house with wrap around porch. Surprisingly, it looked pristine. White with navy shutters, a welcoming red door, and gorgeous flowers gracing its beds. When she pulled up towards the front and parked next to Alice, she watched as an orange tabby cat lazily draped itself over the porch banister, its tail twitching in welcome as Alice began to climb the few steps leading to the front door. Julia brushed her hand over its soft fur and smiled as it purred, rising to its feet to give a long stretch before jumping to the porch and winding around her ankles. Alice opened the screen door and tapped her knuckles on the front door before turning the knob and letting herself inside. "Graham!" she yelled, Julia cringing at the piercing twang.

Stomps on stairs carried from the other room and the tall man stepped into the room. He'd showered, his hair still damp, and slightly curling behind his ears and across his forehead. He was clean shaven, his jaw firm and defined, giving him an edge even when relaxed. His eyes, a deep blue, narrowed when they landed on Julia and his face turned sour. "What now?" he asked.

"Calm your tatas." Alice pointed to his hand. "You take something for the pain yet?"

"No. I don't need to."

"Yes, you do," Alice ordered.

"It's nothing I can't handle."

"Tough guy, huh?" She reached forward and squeezed his hand a few inches above her stitches. He hissed and growled like an angry bear, his eyes sparking tamed fury. "Right. So here we go." Alice butted past him into the kitchen and opened the far cabinet. Her familiarity with the place intrigued Julia, considering her friend had never mentioned the ranch or the lineup of handsome men she seemed so familiar with. Julia felt the heat of his stare before she even looked his direction. When she did, Julia met Graham's gaze straight on.

"I'd listen to her if I were you," she told him. "or she'll pester you for hours."

Her comment caused a twitch in his lips before he grew serious again, the small change in expression so fleeting she already questioned whether or not it'd actually happened.

"Alice has always been a stubborn—"

"Lady," Alice finished for him, shoving a glass of water in his good hand and holding two pain killers in her open palm for him to take.

"Right. *Lady*." Graham tossed back the pills and took a long gulp of water to wash them down. "Happy now?"

"Yes. For now. I'll be back by tomorrow to check for infection."

"It's fine, Al. Leave it be. Besides, we've got to move the cows and calves out to pasture." He froze, his face turning serious as he glanced at his watch. He stormed to the front door and yanked it open. "Lawrence! Hayes!"

His brother Seth poked his head around the side of the house, a water hose in his hand. "What's up?"

"Not you," Graham told him. "Where are the others?"

"The barn. Why?"

"Y'all pair up those calves?"

"Lawrence was going to do that here in a bit, I believe."

"Well he can't do it alone." Graham stormed back into the house and grabbed his boots by the door and flopped into a chair at the small dining table.

"Graham, the others can handle pairing the calves," Alice stated calmly. "I'll even swing by the barn to remind them. *If* they haven't already done it, which I'm sure they have."

"I better check. Where'd you put that clipboard?"

"Lawrence has it."

Graham nodded as he fitted the last of his boots on and stood. He wore a pair of clean jeans and white undershirt that seemed too bright considering the work he'd been doing earlier. Julia wondered if it was new or just washed in straight bleach day after day. *Probably the latter*, she mused. When he stood, he towered over both women, and Julia couldn't help the female response of measuring him up from his boots all the way to his unruly hair. He was a sight, and a delicious one at that, if she were being honest. But the hard set of the jaw carried into his shoulders and she wondered if the man ever truly relaxed. He opened the door as the other three brothers that'd helped at the pens were clearing the front steps.

"We got'em, Graham." Lawrence, Julia assumed, answered before the question was asked. He handed the clipboard to Graham. "All paired off and are doing fine."

"Good."

Lawrence slipped his hat off his head and held a hand towards Julia. "I apologize, ma'am, for not introducing myself earlier. I'm Lawrence. Lawrence Hastings. Thank you for that... delicious lunch earlier."

Julia grinned and accepted his hand, knowing he'd suffered through his sandwich like the others. But she thought it sweet that he'd try to smooth over the debacle.

"Julia McComas."

"Nice to meet you." Lawrence placed his hat back on his head as Hayes introduced himself in the same manner. Clint, having already tried to charm her by helping lift her cooler earlier, just stood to the side and openly checked her out.

"Where's Cal?" Graham asked.

"Over in the east pasture still. On the dozer," Hayes replied.

"Good. Maybe one of us can get a full day's work in. You talk to Philip yet?"

"No." Lawrence took the question. "He's on my list. I gotta go into town tomorrow so I figured I'd swing by the feed store then."

"Fine," Graham agreed. "Just make sure it's about ten tons. He should be able to bulk order that for us."

"I know," Lawrence replied, challenging his older brother's hard stare.

Surprisingly, Graham moved on. "Tomorrow morning, we'll start bustling them out of the trap. Seth driving the feed truck. Rest of us on horseback."

"Got it." Hayes nodded as he listened.

"Calvin can finish up the east pasture. We should be able to handle the cows ourselves."

"Got it," Hayes repeated. "Now can we go eat something. I'm starving." His face blanched as he realized he let his comment slip in front of Julia. A pink tinge colored his cheeks as he cleared his throat and mumbled something about a shower first.

Julia bit back a smile. She was sorry to have disappointed them all, but she loved the way they attempted to wash over the incident. It was charming, in an odd way. All of them but Graham. He just seemed to boss everyone around. "I'm sorry I didn't buy the barbecue."

"Oh, it's alright, ma'am." Hayes, still embarrassed by his slip up, took a step down the steps. "We appreciate you feeding us anyway."

"As you should," Alice agreed. "Now, I'm taking my friend to the bustling town of Parks and introducing her to Sloppy's steak tonight. Any of you want to join us for supper later, come on by."

"Steak?" Seth's head whipped around the side of the house.

"Nosey." Alice grinned. "Yes. We'll be there at six."

"We're busy," Graham reported, and all the brothers looked at him as if he were crazy. "And we have an early morning tomorrow since we weren't able to finish up today."

Alice rolled her eyes. "It's three in the afternoon, Graham. Take a nap."

Lawrence bit back a grin. "Steak sounds good. Count me in."

Defying his brother seemed to please Lawrence more than the promise of steak. Julia watched as he winked towards Graham and accepted the harsh glare in response with a wide grin of his own.

"You can stay at home and rest that hand," Alice told him. "Wouldn't hurt to put another dose of antibiotic ointment on there tonight."

"I know how to take care of a cut," Graham mumbled.

"Right." Clint guffawed. "Like that time you almost lost your foot. You did a real good job taking care of "a cut" then."

The other brothers grinned as Graham silently took their teasing.

Alice issued a reassuring pat on his shoulder. "We'll have a beer in your honor, sour puss."

"That I will," Clint agreed. "But I gotta go take care of myself if I'm to be in on makin' an appearance in town." He held his dirty shirt away from his body and brushed away a few crusty crumbs of dried manure. Julia's nose curled as she watched the dark speckles land on the clean floor.

"Might want to shave that face too." Alice rubbed her hand over his rough exterior. "Poor Julia thought she'd stumbled upon a bunch of cavemen."

Clint rubbed his jaw, and Julia noticed the other three brothers do the same, as though they hadn't even considered their unruly beards an eyesore. Graham was the only bare face in the bunch, and something told Julia he was the only one who kept his face clean.

"Been awhile since we've been to town," Hayes defended. "Not even to church. Hadn't had much of a reason to shave."

"Well, now you do. If you want to be seen in public with Julia and me, you need to look the part of a gentleman."

"Scolding us is her spiritual gift," Seth whispered to Julia and accepted the punch to his shoulder in good humor as Alice motioned towards the door.

"Come on, Julia. Let's leave these brutes to their clean up duty. Six 'o clock. Sloppy's," she repeated to them. "Don't be late or you'll miss your chance of buying Julia her first drink in Parks."

Lawrence reached and opened the door for the women as they made their way towards their separate vehicles. Julia climbed into her little red Honda and shut the door.

"She's a pretty thing, isn't she?" Lawrence commented as they all waved to send the ladies off.

"Pretty?" Seth whistled. "Did you see those legs?"

"I saw them first," Clint said.

"No way, man. I'm the one who saved her from the cow. Dibs."

Lawrence shook his head on a laugh. "Something tells me Ms. Julia doesn't have time for ol' rednecks like us. Right, Graham?"

Graham grunted as he stalked over to the refrigerator and grabbed himself a beer.

Clapping his hands together, Hayes stepped towards the door. "Whether I got a shot with the beautiful new face or not doesn't matter. I'm going to get myself cleaned up so I can enjoy a tantalizing evening with a big, juicy steak. See you losers later." He hustled down the steps towards his truck and encouraged a mass exodus of the remaining brothers as they all left Graham standing on the porch, hungry, annoyed, and sore.

∞

He had to admit he was a bit annoyed to be sitting at home while his brothers were to indulge in a nice meal in town. He watched as they headed to Parks, no doubt dressed in their best shirts and boots to impress Julia. He walked over to the refrigerator and rummaged inside for something to scrounge up for dinner. He could have sworn he'd had enough leftover spaghetti to last him a couple days. Growling, he knew the culprit who'd raided his refrigerator. Calvin. Guess he couldn't blame his brother for sneaking in and grabbing a bite to eat. He'd been working hard on the dozer most of the day clearing the fence line in the east pasture. Work that would drive Graham nuts, being contained on a piece of machinery all day. However, that put him at a disadvantage for dinner. Like his brothers, he hadn't ventured to town in a couple of weeks and groceries were slim. He'd finished off his last beer when Alice was still here, and he had a choice of a tomato sandwich, a jar of pickles, or he needed to make a trip to town for groceries. Or a steak. Which, when he thought about it, had his stomach grumbling in its favor.

His pride could suffer an evening with Alice and Julia if it meant his stomach would be full.

It took all but five minutes for him to find a clean button up shirt and slip his boots on. He wasn't about to primp for Julia like his brothers had. He'd wear what he had. Yes, his boots were a bit dirty, but it was just Sloppy's. He'd be shocked if Julia would even step foot inside the building after her reaction to the barbecue joint in Sheffield. Reaching for his keys, he walked out of the house and ran a hand down the back of Curly, his cat, and headed to his truck.

The twenty miles into Parks never seemed like enough time for him to brace himself for socialization. He hated making trips to town, even if it was to grab a good meal with family and friends. He liked his secluded life on the ranch. No visitors unless he planned for them. No gossipers. No pretty women from out of town. Usually, anyway. He pulled into the parking lot of Sloppy's and spotted Alice's truck, Hayes's truck, and Calvin's truck as well. He assumed the other brothers carpooled with one or the other. The gravel crunched under his boots as he walked towards the door. Roughneck Randy sat on the porch in his old wooden chair with its seat cushion caving through to the porch. He beamed up at Graham and accepted the handshake. "Randy," he greeted.

"How's the farm?" The man's toothless grin spit more than spoke, but he was a Parks staple, and Graham always believed in valuing those who'd helped build up the community. And back in his prime, Roughneck Randy, as the man was so affectionately called, did just that. He was but a mere shadow of the man he used to be, but his pride in Parks and the people were what seemed to stabilize him. And Sloppy was kind enough to let the old man be on the front porch of her restaurant day in and day out.

"Doing good. Worked calves this mornin'."

"That how you got that there band-aid?"

The large white wrapping around Graham's hand was a bit more than just a band-aid. "It is. Seth dropped the leg at the first sight of a pretty female and nearly lost my hand."

"I saw said female." Randy crossed his arms and nodded. "I'd drop the leg too if she were in my arena." His shoulders shook as his wheezy laugh had Graham smiling. "What you fellas get, closin' yourselves off out there. See a pretty face and lose your minds. Ya need more practice around the other sex. And church don't count." He narrowed his gaze at Graham and nodded for him to head inside. "Now treat the lady to a drink, on me." Randy didn't offer the money for said drink, just his typical nod of entrance.

Graham stepped inside and slipped his hat from his head as he searched the room for his brothers. He heard the laughter and immediately looked to the left. Sloppy waved from behind the bar as she swiped a towel over the overly polished wood. "Hey Slop, how's it going?"

"Good, Graham. Heard about your accident today." She grimaced when she eyed his hand. "You going to live?"

He smirked as he accepted the cold bottle of beer she slid across to him. "Much to everyone's disappointment, I think so."

She grinned. "That's good. Seth wasn't too sure if he would after today."

"His fate is still in question," Graham admitted unforgivingly.

"Don't be too hard on him. He was a hero. Let him bask in that for at least a few days." Grinning, she nodded towards the table where his family sat. "She's real pretty."

"You're real pretty," Graham complimented and had Sloppy rolling her eyes.

"And don't you forget it."

Graham glanced at her name tag. "Ruby, is it?"

"So my birth certificate says."

"Don't recall ever seeing you wear your actual name before."

"Well, maybe I'm tired of people calling me Sloppy." She smiled, her red lips freshly painted.

"You haven't been sloppy since you were fourteen years old. It's not your fault you live in Parks and nicknames seem to stick."

"True. Guess I need to branch out then."

Graham tilted his head. "You thinkin' about it?"

"The thought has crossed my mind," Ruby admitted. "But then what would I do with this place and old Randy?"

Graham shrugged. "He's a grown man."

"Right." Ruby leaned on her elbows, her dark, pixie cut hair swooped to the side of her face. She'd always struck Graham as a poisonous fairy. A dainty girl with a short crop of black hair, creamy skin, and that odd style of wearing bold colors on her lips and eye lids. To him, Ruby had always been the little girl that tagged along after them in school. Unruly hair, skinned knees, and stained dresses. "Well, I can tell you what a few grown men are doing right now, and that's making fools of themselves over the newcomer. Go humble them, Graham, before they embarrass the family name." She winked and walked down the bar to another local customer.

He grabbed his hat and beer and walked towards his family. Alice spotted him first, her eyes widening a small fraction before a slow smile crept over her face. "Well, well, well, look who decided to join us."

Her comment had everyone else glancing his direction. Everyone smiled minus one person: Julia. She seemed to shrink back into her chair and that surprised him. He wasn't sure how he felt about a woman being scared of him, and he sensed that from across the room as his eyes met hers. Wariness watched his every move as he walked towards the table. He tugged on Seth's collar, his youngest brother voicing a protest as Graham plucked him out of his seat at the head of the table and next to Julia and nudged him further down the table. Graham eased into the chair, his knees slightly bumping the underside of the table.

Alice laughed at Julia's surprise of him sitting beside her. Graham extended his good hand towards Julia. She hesitated but then slipped hers into his. "Graham Hastings. Don't think we've had a proper introduction." He waited patiently as she just stared at him as if he'd dropped down from another planet. She blinked, and then forced a polite smile. "Julia McComas. It's nice to meet you, Graham."

"And what changed your mind?" Alice asked.

Graham pinned a pointed gaze at his brother Calvin. "I was hungry."

Calvin rubbed his stomach. "Thanks for the spaghetti earlier."

"Jerk." Graham reached for the menu on the table and flipped through it, already knowing what he wanted.

"We haven't ordered yet," Alice reported. "We were waiting for you to get here."

Graham glanced up. "How'd you know I'd come?"

She nodded towards Calvin. "He confessed and we knew you'd bite the bullet for a good steak."

"Seems I'm predictable."

"I'd hardly say that," Julia mumbled as she took a sip of her own drink. He turned and quirked a brow at her before turning back to his menu.

"Guess I'll throw you all off tonight, then, and say that I'm buyin'."

Seth and Clint hooted and held up a hand towards Sloppy at the bar for another round of drinks.

"Don't go crazy," Graham warned them.

"You offered," Clint reminded him.

"True. But we have to move cows tomorrow. I don't want you fools falling out of the saddle."

"Turn it off, Graham," Lawrence warned. "Just be generous and move on."

Taking his brother's advice, Graham decided it wouldn't be so bad to just enjoy the company and a good dinner. He watched Clint toss back the rest of his beer when Ruby walked up with the next round. *Maybe.*

—H—

Chapter Three

"*And what will it be,* Graham?" Ruby asked, pen and pad in hand.

"Steak. Medium rare. And whatever else you want to put with it."

Ruby nodded and jotted down his order. She looked to Julia. "And you, sweetie?"

"Same. Please."

"It's a big steak. We offer half steaks," Ruby offered.

"I'm good," Julia assured her. "I like steak."

"Atta girl." Ruby winked and moved on down. She tapped her elbow against Lawrence's head to get his attention, the brother immediately reciting his dish of choice.

"You like steak, but you bought vegan sandwiches for lunch?"

"I have varied tastes. Do you guys come here often?" Julia asked Graham.

"Yes. When we can. Sloppy's a family friend." He nodded towards Ruby.

"That's Sloppy?" Julia's eyes widened. "She doesn't look sloppy to me. She's beautiful."

"That she is. But like all people, she had an awkward stage... hers just happened to be from age zero to fourteen."

"And the nickname stuck," Julia finished, and he nodded.

"Well, I'm glad to see she embraces it. Not many people would."

"It's how people know her around here. Few really know her real name."

"And what about you?"

"What about me?"

"Do you know her real name?" Julia asked.

"Of course I do." He looked offended.

"And what is it?"

"Ruby Cole."

Julia smiled in appreciation. "So why did you sit beside me? After today I figured you would want to boot me out of Parks forever."

"This is the head of the table." He pointed to his chair.

"And?"

"And I'm the head of the family." He pointed to his brothers. "I always sit at the head of the table."

"Seriously?" she asked, knowing the answer. His face was overly serious, as if her question was completely preposterous.

"Why wouldn't I be?"

"Just seems a bit old fashioned, I guess."

He shrugged. "Just how it's been."

"Hey Julia, good news, Calvin's going to come check out my air conditioner."

"Oh, good." Relief washed over her face.

"What's wrong with your AC?" Graham asked.

"My window unit's acting up. My house is as hot as Hades' first flirtation with flames. We about died just changing clothes to come here. It's miserable in the house."

"Keep telling you to have your house converted to central air and heat. You sweat all summer and 'bout freeze all winter because of that stupid unit," Graham muttered.

"But then I wouldn't be able to call upon a Hastings brother to come to my rescue," Alice smirked. "You know I have to do my part to make you guys feel special every once in a while."

Julia grinned at her friend and then turned to see Graham's reaction. Absolutely no emotion could be read on his face. The man was an iron mask. Did he ever smile? Or laugh?

"I would have fixed it for ya, Al," Seth offered.

"No thanks. You fixed it last time... a week ago, and yet, here we are."

The brothers laughed as Seth sheepishly shrugged. He looked at his watch. "Did anyone tell Philip we were eatin' in town tonight?"

None of the brothers acknowledged his question.

"Well, ain't that a shame." Seth whipped out his cell phone. "He'd be awfully disappointed to miss out on a steak on Graham's tab."

"I think he had a date in Sheffield." Clint interrupted.

"A date?" Hayes' brows rose. "When did Philip start datin'?"

"Does it matter?" Alice asked. "Good for him. Might do you all some good to find a girl to take out every now and then. Teach ya'll some manners."

"Don't have time for women," Lawrence admitted with a disappointed frown. "At least, no time to drive and meet any."

"It's not that far to Sheffield," Julia encouraged.

"I'm not talking about Sheffield," Lawrence stated. "That town's not much bigger than Parks. If we wanted to find a good woman, we'd have to go farther than 60 miles."

"Unless a good woman came to you," Julia replied. Several heads turned her direction and Graham's brow arched at her response to his brother. She blushed. "I didn't mean me. I just meant that maybe... I don't know... one will turn up one day. Soon. And there's always Alice. She's single."

Alice choked back a sip of her drink and Hayes lightly patted her on the back.

"They always say to never settle," Lawrence said. "And, well, Alice would be settling if she chose one of us. She deserves the best."

"Awe, thanks Lawrence." Alice beamed across the table. "And that mentality right there is what would make you a delightful catch for any woman."

"Women are a distraction," Graham reminded his brother.

Julia turned in surprise. "A distraction? That's a bit rude."

"Really?" he asked, holding up his hand. "Would I have this if you hadn't distracted Seth earlier today? Would the cow have charged if you hadn't distracted her?"

Julia fumbled over what to say. "Well, you were removing its... well, you were being mean to the calf. I'd be upset if that were happening to my baby. Wouldn't you?"

"There's a purpose for it. We don't do it to be mean," Graham added bluntly. "Lowers the testosterone production, helps them gain weight better, which in turn helps them build up more internal intermuscular fat resulting in a better grade of meat. You said you like steak. How do you think a good quality steak comes about?"

Miffed, but somewhat appeased that there was an actual reason behind what she'd witnessed earlier, she soaked in the cocky tilt to his head as he crossed his arms in challenge.

"Alright, well you don't have to be arrogant about it."

He cocked his dark brow. "Not arrogant, educated. There's a difference. Arrogance would be stomping into a cow pen like you own the place."

Julia slapped his arm with impressive force. Her face registered her surprise at the motion and had everyone at the table watching the two of them.

"I'm so sorry about that." She shifted away from Graham. Embarrassed, she tucked her hair behind her ear and reached for her drink to take a sip and cool her temper.

"I can take a hit," Graham added.

"He's used to women slapping him," Clint teased, receiving the steady glare his oldest brother must have mastered at birth.

"Never been slapped. That's your department."

Clint flushed slightly and then shrugged. "It's true. But only twice."

A cell phone jingled and had them all staring at Alice. She glanced at the caller id and groaned. "It's the office line patching through. Gotta take this." She slipped away from the table and was back in seconds. "Gotta go. Seems I'll be helping deliver two foals tonight."

"But what about your dinner? And you've been drinking," Julia pointed out.

"Nope. It's a vanilla coke." Alice smiled. "I had a feeling the Jepsons' mare would pop any day, so I've played it safe. Just have Sloppy box mine up and put it in the fridge. Calvin will drive you to my place and fix the AC tonight." She looked to the brother for confirmation and he nodded.

"But—" Julia's eyes pleaded with her friend not to leave, but Alice was already shouting her orders to Sloppy about her meal and pushing her chair under the table.

"See you later. Don't wait up. If I come home tonight, it will be super late. I may just crash on a cot in the barn at the Jepsons' and come home tomorrow, depending on how the night goes. You'll be fine." She flashed a quick smile before snatching her purse from under the table.

"But—" Julia tried again and was talking to air. Alice was gone in a whirl.

It was her first night in the strange town. She was sitting at a table with six strange men, one of whom would be taking her to Alice's house later. Nothing about her first night in Parks seemed *fine*. Keeping her feelings to herself, Julia forced a smile as Clint carried on about the safety of Parks. But deep down, Julia battled frustration and nerves about spending her first night alone.

∞

"Look, if you need anything, Sloppy lives just around the corner." Graham pointed to a small house up the street from Alice's.

Alice lived in a small, efficiency style home. One bedroom, one bathroom, an open concept kitchen, living, and dining area that consisted of a couch that folded out into the bed Julia would be sleeping on for the next couple of weeks. The house was old, built years ago by a roughneck working the oilfields in order to avoid hotel costs. It needed a decent paint job, some new porch steps, and lots of small fixer upper jobs. But despite those few things, the place had charm. Graham always liked the little space and wondered why Sloppy didn't use it instead of her house up the street since it was located behind her restaurant. But Sloppy needed some space, he guessed.

He pointed to Calvin putting his toolbox back into the bed of his truck. "Looks like Cal's done with the AC." Having left as soon as he'd finished his steak, Calvin had forgotten his duty of delivering Julia back to Alice's house. So Graham, attempting to be a gentleman, made the offer. She'd accepted with great reluctance, but seemed to weigh her options amongst all the brothers and found him the best one. That was at least encouraging, since his brothers were in no shape to entertain female company after a few beers.

Graham rolled down his window and Cal walked up. "Hate to tell you this, Julia, but that AC is completely busted. There's no saving it."

"Are you sure?" Graham asked.

Calvin narrowed his eyes. "Definitely yes. It's smoked. I'd suggest calling Mrs. Haymill to see if she can put you up for the night over at the Whippoorwill."

"That place is a dump," Graham muttered.

Cal shrugged. "That or sweat it out for tonight and maybe Alice can get a new unit tomorrow. I already called her with the news."

Julia wrung her hands in her lap.

Graham waited patiently, though he was aware of the lateness of the hour and his early morning. And his hand, geez, his hand was killing him.

"Well, I'm sure one night won't be too bad." Julia shouldered her purse and took her first cautious step out of the truck. A loud crash had her jumping back inside. "What was that?"

"Probably a coon." Graham waved away her concern. "Sloppy's dumpsters are just over there. I'm sure there's just a nightly visitor."

"A raccoon?" Julia took a deep breath and nodded. "You're probably right. No reason to worry."

"I also told Alice her porch lights were out. Both. Front and back." Cal shook his head in bewilderment. "And naturally she doesn't have any extra bulbs. I don't have any on me, either. That woman has no clue when it comes to maintenance."

"It is rather dark," Julia's voice squeaked as her eyes surveyed the small shabby house and the shadows surrounding it.

"Look, if you're scared, Sloppy's on the corner, or if it makes you feel better, here." Graham grabbed an old receipt off his dash and jotted down his phone number. "Here," he said again, nudging it towards her. "But only if you're terrified and think someone is breaking in."

"Is that common around here?" Panic lit her eyes and he immediately regretted his choice of words.

"No."

"Oh, good. Okay." She accepted the slip of paper. "Thank you. And thank you for the ride." She slipped from his passenger seat and offered a small smile towards Cal. She turned briskly at the sound of Graham shifting his truck into gear. "Wait." She placed a hand on the windowsill of the passenger side. "Could you just... wait until I get inside?"

Cal tapped Graham's windowsill and smiled. "I'm out of here. See you in the morning. Night, Julia."

"Goodnight, Cal. Thank you." He tipped his hat and climbed into his truck.

"Well..." Graham nodded towards the house and Julia visibly inhaled a deep breath.

"Right. Here I go." She reluctantly released his truck and walked to the sagging porch. Turning the knob, she let herself inside and flipped on the lamp by the door. She offered a brief wave before closing the door and no doubt locking it as best she could and then blocking it with every piece of furniture she could get her hands on. Graham shook his head and chuckled. "City girls." He started to turn the wheel when the door to the house flew open and Julia sprinted outside in pure terror. Graham threw the truck in park and hopped out, Julia slamming into him as he rounded the hood. He caught her by the shoulders.

"There's a thing in there! A-a-creature! In the kitchen!" She pointed a shaky finger, her breaths heavy as she ducked under his arm and tucked herself behind him while fisting her hands in the back of his shirt.

"What kind of creature?" Graham asked. "A person? An animal?"

"Animal. Big."

He started to walk forward and her grip on his shirt had him stopping and lightly tapping her hands. She released him, but followed him step for step as he walked up the front porch steps. The sound of breaking glass towards the kitchen had Graham turning. Julia gasped. "What is that thing?" Horrified and disgusted, she gripped the back of his shirt again as he stepped forward.

"Would you let go of me?" He swatted her hands again. "How'm I supposed to help you if you won't let me move?"

"I'm sorry," she whispered. "Just... be careful. I've never seen one of those things before, Graham. It's probably dangerous."

Graham just shook his head as he eyed a laundry basket set to the side of the door with neatly folded clothes inside. He dumped it on the floor and heard another small gasp from Julia at his move before he stealthily walked forward. He quickly lunged forward, and Julia shrieked as he trapped the critter in the basket. He looked around again. "Any cardboard or something flat lyin' around?"

"What? No." Julia looked perplexed as she searched the small house. "What do we do?" She twisted her hands together, her eye never leaving the basket.

"Go out to the dumpsters behind Sloppy's and see if you can find a box."

"What? I'm not going out there. It's dark. And a dumpster."

He rolled his eyes, his hand resting on top of the basket, the animal hissing at him. "Fine. I'll go." He stepped away from the basket and Julia intercepted him.

"Whoa. You can't go. You have to keep th-th-that thing trapped."

He exhaled a heavy sigh and pinched the bridge of his nose. "Julia, it's a 'possum. It's not a raging bull... or cow. You'll be fine." He reached towards her carry-on suitcase and grabbed the handle, placing it securely over the top of the basket. "See, it's not going anywhere."

He walked past her and out the door towards Sloppy's as he heard her mutter, "But that's my bag," and heard her heels crunching on the ground behind him.

"How do you think it got into the house?" she asked.

"Probably through the back screen door. It has a hole the size of Kansas back there."

"But... we have the wooden door open to let air into the house. The screen door is supposed to keep the bugs out. If we close the wooden door, then it will be even hotter in the house."

"Guess you'll have to sweat tonight. And what good is a screen door doing to keep bugs out if it has a giant hole in it?" Graham reached for a cardboard box and began kicking in the sides to break it down flat. Julia followed as he carried it back towards the house.

"Well, I don't know. I just went with what Alice said, since this seems to be a common predicament for her." Julia hugged along behind him and as soon as they entered the house, she grew still and quiet again, for which he was grateful.

He removed her suitcase from atop the basket and set it aside. She quickly intercepted it and rolled it as far from the possum as she could.

Graham began sliding the cardboard beneath the basket, the 'possum hissing but stepping lightly to avoid the intrusion until its feet rested on top of the cardboard. Graham flipped the basket, the critter now inside the basket and covered with the cardboard. He carried it out the screen door and towards the alleyway. Naturally, Julia followed.

He removed the cardboard and let the animal free down the side of the alley. They watched as it sniffed and rummaged its way along. "You just let it go?" she asked. "Aren't we supposed to call animal control or something?"

"No. It's a 'possum. It's not a stray dog. Besides, they're helpful critters. They eat mosquitos and bugs. Maybe I should have left him in the house considering the hole in the door. He could help with the bug problem you're so worried about. They're pretty harmless critters. They just get scared easily."

"And probably carry about a thousand diseases."

"As do some humans too, so best not to judge."

Julia crossed her arms and narrowed her eyes. "That's gross, Graham."

"But true." He pointed a finger in the air as he walked back to the house and began rummaging in a drawer in the kitchen. Not finding what he was after, he stalked back to his truck and opened his tool chest on the back.

"What are you looking for?" Julia asked, her short, quick steps following him everywhere he went.

He held up a roll of duct tape. "Going to patch your screen door. Then you can leave it open for air. How's that?"

"I can't leave it open now." Julia adamantly shook her head. "What if another creature decides to come into the house?"

"The hole will be blocked. They can't get in."

"They could just chew through the wire, couldn't they?"

"Possibly. But I doubt they will. They don't want to be around people."

"But what about people. That door is hardly safe to leave open all night long when I'm by myself."

"No one's going to bother you," Graham assured her as he began taping the door. Long strip after long strip, he finally felt it was secure enough to hold a few weeks until Alice wrapped her mind around the fact her house was falling apart and needed some TLC.

"How can you be sure?"

"Because I know the people of this town."

"But what if there's a drifter?"

He groaned and stood to his feet and faced her. "Look, I know you're not used to life outside of the city, but around here, people mind their own business. No one's going to bother you."

"But—"

"No buts. Now, goodnight."

"Graham—" She scurried after him to the front door.

"What?" His patience was wearing thin, and he was about to slam his head into the wall if she delayed his taking a strong painkiller any longer.

"Thank you," she quietly said and ducked her head.

"You're welcome. Now, can I go home?" He waited for her to look up at him.

She finally met his gaze and nodded.

"Good. I'm exhausted. And my hand is killing me."

She grimaced. "I didn't think of that. I'm sorry. I could take a look at it if you want."

"Are you a doctor?"

"No."

"Then I'm good, thanks."

She huffed and crossed her arms. "I just meant I could check your bandage and help you wrap it in a fresh one. I do know how to do that."

"Good to know, but I'm good. Night." He let himself out and prayed he'd make it all the way home before his cell phone rang. What was he thinking giving that woman his number? He rubbed a hand over his tired face and breathed a sigh of relief when he turned the corner to head out of town.

H

Chapter Four

Laughter had been all she'd heard all morning from Alice since she'd walked in at the crack of dawn with her vet bag. Julia knew she looked a fright; the night was miserable and had clearly stamped itself across her face and under her eyes. She'd sweated every drop of water in her body, or so it felt. And she barely shut her eyes due to sounds of dumpster diving creatures and a creak at the door all night long. Despite Graham's patchwork in the screen door, she swatted away mosquitos most of the night. She'd attempted to hide under the covers only to sweat some more, and then would toss away the sheets only to be bitten by bugs again; an endless cycle that kept sleep at bay. It was a no-win situation that left her wide-eyed, annoyed, and scared out of her mind the entire night. Now she ached for a cup of decent coffee, not the sludge sinking to the bottom of the pot that Alice had made when she got home. She could smell the caramel flavored cream steaming from her mug as if she were sitting outside on the patio of her favorite Santa Fe coffee shop. Only a cackle of laughter brought her back to her senses.

"You don't look so fantastic either." Julia narrowed her gaze at her friend and shuffled towards the refrigerator, praying Alice at least had some juice to quench her thirst until Sloppy's opened and Julia could beg for a decent cup of joe.

"I slept in a barn. You slept in a house."

"Oh, is that what you call this?" Julia pointed around. "I had a visitor last night. A possum, according to Graham. And then about a million mosquitos. And I'm pretty sure Satan himself decided those were not enough and sent me an exciting heat wave from hell to make my night more enjoyable."

Alice snickered as she grabbed a bag of powdered donuts from her pantry and plopped down at her dinette table and began to munch. "Welcome to Parks."

"Yes, well, so far my trip has not kicked off to a great start."

Alice's face sobered. "Sorry about that. Life here is a bit different than Santa Fe. I didn't realize Graham came by." Her leading tone had Julia turning from the fridge with a carton of eggs in her hand.

"He drove me home from Sloppy's."

Alice pointed to the building across from her house. "That Sloppy's? The one that is walking distance from my house?" She quirked an eyebrow.

"It was dark. And you asked Calvin to drive me, don't you remember?"

"That's because I knew Calvin would need tools from his truck. Graham seriously drove you a hundred feet?" She unleashed a fit of giggles. "I bet he thoroughly enjoyed that."

"I'm not sure that man enjoys anything," Julia reported. "But he was nice enough to do it, and thank the Lord he did, because you had a 'possum *in your house!*"

"I bet he loved playing the part of hero." Sarcasm dripped from Alice's voice as she continued to smile at the thought of Graham having to tend to her friend. "I have to head over there here in a few if you want to join?"

"Seriously?" Julia asked. "What for?"

"It's my day off."

"And?"

"And I usually go out to the 7H to see if I can help, mostly with the gardening. Only Seth and Lawrence tend to take care of the landscaping and garden plot."

"And that's how you spend your day off?"

"I like being outside," Alice defended. "Besides, it will be fun. You can see how the ranch operates on a day to day basis."

"Look, I didn't realize I would be traipsing around a ranch during my stay. I didn't exactly bring work clothes with me." Julia nibbled her bottom lip as she began pulling different clothing options from her bag. She held up a button-up blouse covered in small flowers with billowing sleeves.

"Perfect. Wear it with jeans," Alice said. "And close-toed shoes."

Julia nodded and quickly changed. She still felt slightly sticky but her cold shower did nothing more than irritate her further. She made sure to spray an extra squirt of perfume to cover any sweat smells that might still linger.

"You've always been so prissy." Alice stood and walked to her closet and pulled out a fresh plaid shirt and put it on. She didn't bother with changing her jeans, socks, or boots.

"And I forgot how tomboy you were," Julia smirked. "Just so you know, I think the Hastings brothers intend to lecture you when they see you."

"On what?"

"The condition of your house. The lightbulbs, the door, the AC. At least, Calvin seemed a little aggravated you hadn't taken care of those things."

Alice waved away the concern. "Calvin's always a stickler when it comes to maintenance. That's why he's the heavy machine operator out at the ranch. He's the only one who will tend to those hunks of metal like tender babies. It wounds his heart to see any type of building or machine in need of care."

"Well, can we at least grab a cup of coffee on the way there?" Julia asked.

Alice pointed to the pot plugged into the wall next to the microwave.

"That is not coffee."

Sighing, Alice walked towards the door. "Sloppy's doesn't open for another hour. I'm sure Graham will have some on. Let's go."

∞

"About time you showed up." Seth grinned as he walked towards Alice's car and opened the door for Julia. He tipped his hat. "Morning."

"You seem awfully chipper for having to wake up early." Alice jabbed him with her elbow as they walked towards the garden.

"I am. I did not have to work the cattle this morning."

"Graham still punishing you for yesterday?" Alice asked.

"Yes. Though I don't consider it much of a punishment." Seth grinned. "The last thing I wanted this morning was to drive the feed truck."

"Don't blame you. Though I'm surprised he changed his mind." She pointed to Julia. "I brought help this morning."

"I see that. Pretty help too." He winked.

"But I promised her a decent cup of coffee before work."

"Graham's got some in the house. He probably left the pot on. Help yourself."

Alice led the way and the women diverted their steps towards the house.

The front door opened moments after they'd poured themselves each a cup of coffee and Graham stormed inside, oblivious to both of them as he headed towards a washroom by the stairwell. They heard a loud hiss as the sink ran water.

Alice walked towards the room. "Slip a stitch?"

Graham jumped, knocking over the bottle of disinfectant he'd sat on the edge of the sink. "What the—"

"Morning." Alice grinned. "Thanks for the coffee." She held up her mug. "What happened?"

"I ripped a stitch or two, I guess."

"Were you wearing gloves?"

"I can't, obviously, because of this bulky bandage you put on here."

"Cry me a river." Alice stepped forward and eyed his hand.

"Two days in a row this hand is keeping me from doing my work," Graham growled.

"Then you should be more careful."

"Okay, Momma."

She snorted as she pointed to the kitchen. "Go to the table. I'll get my kit."

Graham walked towards the kitchen, his steps halting as he spotted Julia holding a cup of coffee in both hands and staring out the window above the sink. The light filtered through the blinds and danced its rays upon her dark hair. She turned and flushed, realizing she'd been caught standing in his house drinking his coffee.

"Morning, Graham."

He pulled a chair away from the table and sat as Alice darted outside to her truck.

Julia glanced at his hand. "Oh no." She rushed towards him and sat next to him, reaching towards his wounded hand. He jerked it away from her touch and she held up her hands in peace. "Sorry. I'm not going to touch it. What happened?"

"Reins just dug in wrong, I guess."

"Can I get you something? A painkiller? Some water? Coffee?"

"Is there any left?" he asked, and she flushed again.

"Yes. Thank you, by the way, for saving Alice's life this morning."

"And how did I manage that?" he asked.

"By having decent coffee."

His lips quirked. "No problem. How was your first night in Parks?"

Surprise lit her face at his question before she diverted her gaze and cleared her throat. "It was fine."

"That good, huh?" A deep rumble had her looking at him again in wonder as he chuckled.

"It was awful," she admitted. "I didn't sleep a wink."

His smirk melted into a full smile at her suffering and she nudged his shoulder. "It's not funny. I was terrified. And hot. And itchy."

His face lifted as he belted a laugh that had Alice freezing in the doorway. "Well, well, well. He does have a bright side every now and then."

Graham quickly sobered. "Julia was just regaling me with her adventures of the night."

"Yes, she is being quite dramatic," Alice teased and accepted the slap to her arm from Julia as she sat on the other side of Graham and reached for his hand.

"What brings you two here this morning?"

"Day off," Alice said and he nodded.

"Well, Seth could use the help. Lawrence is heading into town to order feed from Philip, so he's a bit short-handed."

"Why doesn't Lawrence just call Philip?" Alice asked.

"Seems our brother is avoiding the phone these days."

"Can't blame him."

Graham harrumphed. "I'm a joy to talk to on the phone, thank you very much."

"Oh, I'm sure you are." Alice smirked at Julia. "Thanks for helping Julia out last night. I hear you guys were almost attacked by a 'possum."

"It was a close call," he agreed and shot a quick glance at Julia as she looked heavenward.

"Yes, both of you tease me about it. All I know is that I can't do it two nights in a row. I'm sorry," She looked to Alice. "but I can't." She looked away before they could see her frustration.

Alice must have sensed it anyway because she looked to Graham and grimaced.

"You can use the guest house if you want," Graham offered.

"What?" both women asked in unison.

"The guest house." He pointed to a small white building out the window. "It's not much bigger than Alice's place, but there are no holes in the door. And you will have AC. You're welcome to stay there too, Al. If you want."

"And drive twice the distance to Sheffield? No thanks."

"Well, I wouldn't want to stay without Alice. I'm here to visit her." Julia's tone was disappointed, but Graham liked that her focus was on Alice and not herself. "But thank you for the offer."

"Al's here all the time." Graham looked to the vet as she finished tending to his hand.

"I guess you're right. And I guess we could stay until I get a new AC. I'm over in Sheffield tomorrow and will see what they have," Alice reluctantly agreed. "We just need to fetch your bags and I'll grab a few changes of clothes."

"Lawrence is probably about to head to town here soon. Ride with him." Graham stood and grabbed his hat off the table and placed it on his head. "I gotta get back out there." He let them follow him out as he waved down Lawrence as his brother turned to head down the main road towards the highway. Lawrence slowed his truck to a stop.

"Got room for two women in there?" Graham asked.

"Always." Lawrence grinned and tipped his hat to Julia before looking back to his brother.

"They're going to stay at the guest house."

Lawrence's brows rose in surprise. "Alrighty. Load up." He reached across his truck and opened the passenger door.

Graham turned and Alice was already walking around the hood of the truck to climb in. Julia stood near the porch, admiring his horse he'd tied there on his rush into the house. She cautiously placed her hand on its cheek. When the horse did not react, she smiled and brushed it gently, until his horse began nuzzling her hands.

"Well, nothing better than a beautiful woman loving on your horse." Lawrence grinned over at Alice. "You going to break her trance, or you want to gawk at her a bit longer?"

Graham squinted at his brother as he walked over to his horse. "Your ride is leaving."

"Oh." Julia pulled her hands away. "He's beautiful."

"She."

"She's beautiful," she corrected.

"Thanks."

Sighing, Julia looked up at him. He sensed she wanted to say something else, more than likely scold him or insult him, but she held her tongue and just nodded before walking towards the truck. She gave a small wave as Lawrence directed them towards town.

—*H*—

Chapter Five

It was Julia's first introduction to the brother, Philip. He seemed closer to Graham in height than the other brothers, but his slight, lanky frame mirrored more towards Clint. He was handsome, like the others. Dark headed, dark eyes, a *groomed* beard. Life outside of the ranch seemed to treat him well. And she was surprised to find out that he didn't actually live on the ranch. He lived in town. She wasn't aware any of the Hastings brothers ventured away from the ranch.

Lawrence leaned on the counter as he and Philip discussed feed, protein, and something about cake.

"Ten tons of 20% range cubes. And that comes with our friend and family discount, right?" Lawrence asked with a grin.

"As always. I can have the auger truck bring it out tomorrow."

"Good deal."

Julia wasn't quite listening as she sat on a stool and waited patiently by studying what all the store had to offer.

Philip slid her a bottle across the counter. "You'll want some of that on hand if you're staying at the ranch." He grinned as she read the product label.

"Skunk spray?" Concern had her glancing at the brothers.

"Rumor has it there's one that lives behind the guest house. Best be prepared just in case you get sprayed." Philip winked.

"And this will take away the smell?"

"A bit," Philip said.

"We could always dunk you in a barrel of tomato juice," Lawrence offered and both brothers laughed as she curled her nose.

"Possums. Skunks. Anything else I need to worry about?"

"Graham," both brothers said and then laughed at her worried face.

"He's a bear," Philip explained. "And living so close to him... well, let's just say he likes his space."

"I don't plan on knocking on his door every hour of every day," Julia stated.

"But hey, you've already seen that side of him and survived, so you may do alright," Lawrence encouraged.

"Why is he like that?" Julia asked, curious as to why Graham would have a reason for the chip on his shoulder.

Lawrence shrugged as if he'd never thought about it or didn't care one way or the other.

Philip tilted his head and pondered her question. "I think it's the responsibility aspect that does it to him. He's always breathed that ranch, even as kids. And when our Momma and Daddy died, he took it upon himself to make it work. He's the oldest, so he feels obligated to keep it running. Even with the oil money, he's bound and determined to keep that place operating like it's life or death if it doesn't succeed. But he also loves it, so there's no talking him into selling or stopping."

"Been there, done that," Lawrence chuckled as Philip nodded in agreement.

"Really? You guys almost sold it once?"

"No. The conversation ended before it could even get started," Lawrence told her. "Graham's too attached to it. We all are, I guess, except for Philip."

"Hey now." Philip pointed at him. "I love the place. It's just not the life I wanted or want."

"You must love it enough to still be in the same field of sorts." She waved her hand around the place.

"Sort of my compromise." Philip chuckled.

"I see." Though she didn't, but she planned to ask Alice later.

"Philip helps us save a pretty penny by giving us supplies at wholesale." Lawrence placed his hat back on his head and straightened to full height. "He's helpful, in his own way." He shook his brother's hand.

"Well, it was nice to meet you, Philip." Julia shook the man's hand as well. "Maybe I will see you around the next couple of weeks."

"You know where to find me."

Alice walked up to the counter and dumped a handful of items on the counter for Philip to ring up. "I'm hurrying." She matched Lawrence's annoyed stare and fished in her pocket for a wad of cash she tossed on the counter. "How's the girl, Philip?"

He smiled. "Fine."

"When you going to introduce her to the fam?"

"Not for a while."

"Good call," Alice encouraged. "Wouldn't want to scare her away."

"They aren't that bad," Julia defended and had Lawrence draping his arm over her shoulders and kissing her cheek.

"She likes us," he beamed.

She nudged for him to release his hold and he obliged with a sly grin.

"I wouldn't go that far," she corrected him. "I'm just... getting used to all of you."

"And it's only been a day," Philip laughed. "Just wait. Once that charming polish wears off, they get real interesting."

"Polish?" Lawrence cringed. "I am what I am. What you see is what you get."

"Family motto, it would seem," Alice baited. "If you boys tried just in the slightest, you'd all be married by now. Settled down. But instead, you act like a pack of wild wolves and have the hygiene of them too."

"Says the woman who slept in a barn last night," Julia chimed in.

"For the sting!" Lawrence raised his hand for a high five and lowered it upon seeing Julia's serious face. Philip grinned behind the counter.

"Yes, well, a night I don't plan on repeating for a while." Alice took the bag Philip handed her. "Thanks, Philip. Ready?"

Julia offered one last wave and followed Alice out the door, half listening to Lawrence and Alice nag one another about certain grazing conditions in the northwest. Why that was relevant at the moment, Julia didn't know, nor did she quite care. She was exhausted. When they collected her bags and Alice's— well, Alice's empty laundry basket Graham had used for the possum was stuffed with fresh clothes and that's what Alice deemed a suitcase— they were headed out the door and back towards the ranch.

She felt a tap on her leg when they pulled in and realized she'd fallen asleep with her head against the window. Praying she hadn't snored or talked in her sleep, both fears but never confirmed, she slid out of the truck, thankful for a welcoming home to sleep in.

Graham stepped out of the guest house, his good hand stuffed in his pocket and his bandaged hand tucked towards his middle. She knew it had to bother him, especially after he'd torn it open just this morning, but he seemed somewhat... normal. He still wore a scowl, but she'd slowly grown accustomed to that. He'd smiled that morning, and she'd had to check herself when she saw it. It was fleeting but devastatingly handsome. Who knew he had dimples? She didn't. And they only seemed to emerge when he smiled.

He walked up to the truck and hoisted her bags over the side. He eyed Alice's basket and just gave the familiar shake of his head at her habits as he led the way inside. The small white house mirrored the large family home in that it had navy shutters and a red front door. It had a small porch with two wooden rocking chairs and table between them. The potted plants and flower beds gave it a storybook quality that had Julia's hopes rising. She prayed the inside was as nice as the outside and when she walked in, she felt instant relief. It was bright and cheerful. The colors were neutral, but welcoming, with bold touches here and there. She noticed a few western odds and ends, but they meshed well with the overall feel of the place.

"There's one bedroom there." Graham pointed. "And the other there. They share the bathroom."

He started for one bedroom with Julia's bags as Alice carried her basket to the other. Julia followed him. Her room was light and airy. A queen-sized antique bed frame was covered in a pale yellow spread, a quilt draped over the end. A wooden bench sat at the end of the bed and Graham laid her bags on top of it.

"This is beautiful, Graham. Thank you again for letting us stay here."

"No problem. Hasn't been used in a while, but I had Annie swing by and freshen the place up for you."

"Annie?"

"Cleaning lady."

She now understood why it looked the way it did, complete with fresh flowers in a vase on the vanity by the window.

"It's heavenly," Julia admitted.

"I imagine anything would be after your night last night."

"It was interesting, that's for sure," Julia admitted.

"Well, you made it. What doesn't kill you makes you stronger, right?"

"Sometimes," she said. "How's your hand?"

He glanced down at the bandage. "Fine."

She knew that was all she was to get out of him, so she let the subject drop and walked towards the window of the room and gazed out at the view behind the small house. Open pastures as far as the eyes could see. Calm. Peaceful. And surprisingly not freaking her out at the moment.

"Well, I'll leave you to it then." Graham walked back into the main room of the house and intercepted Alice.

"She still awake in there?" Alice asked. "She fell asleep on the way here."

"She's a ghost walkin', Alice. You should know better."

"I know," Alice sighed. "I've just been so busy lately I didn't have time to prep my place for company. It sort of snuck up on me. Thankfully, Julia's always been a tough nut to crack, so she's still here."

"I'm guessing you didn't bring food either."

Alice cringed. "I didn't think about that."

"I figured." Graham walked towards the pantry and opened the door. "I had Annie grab some essentials."

"I'm beginning to think Annie is an angel." Julia's voice had them both startling.

"Some days she is. Been with us a long time. You may see her around. She buzzes in and out periodically. If you need anything, just let her know. She'll take care of it."

"I can't imagine needing anything right now but a hot bath and a nap, and thanks to you, I can do just that. Thank you again." Julia gently placed her hand on his arm, stood on her tiptoes and kissed his cheek.

Graham's neck flushed as he took a step towards the door, placing his hat back on his head. "Don't mention it. See you two around." He walked out without a backwards glance.

"Scared him off already." Alice giggled as they watched him hurry towards the barn, his quick, long strides eating up the distance in short time. He barked something at Seth as he passed the garden, the younger brother offering a wave over his shoulder in acknowledgment.

"He's so tall." Julia continued her perusal as Alice stood to the side amused.

"Oh yeah, and *super* hot."

"Right?" Julia agreed, before realizing what Alice had just said. "Wait, what?"

Alice laughed. "Caught ya. You like Graham."

Baffled, Julia shook her head. "No, not at all. I just appreciate his kindness."

"Kindness, my butt," Alice chuckled. "Or his, I can't quite tell what you're looking at now. Kindness and Graham aren't usually in the same sentence," Alice stated.

"Um, he's letting us stay in his guest house. I'd say that's kind."

"It is. And I'll admit, I'm surprised he offered. But I wouldn't set your hopes on Graham Hastings."

"Who said I was setting my hopes anywhere? I'm only here a couple weeks. I was just... admiring his... build," Julia admitted.

"You mean checkin' him out," Alice pointed out. "Well, I admit, it's hard not to. All of them of are pretty. Long legs, beefy muscles, heads full of hair... potential heartbreakers if they ventured outside of Parks. But all of them are rough around the edges, their manners a bit crude. Course I imagine that's because their momma died when they were rather young and old man Hastings never remarried. The only woman to ever put up with all of them was Annie. Guess you could say she was their mother hen when need be. But she also knew her place."

"They seem to have turned out well enough," Julia added. "And all have been respectful and kind to me since I arrived."

Alice shrugged. "We'll see what you think after a few days out here with them."

"And what about you?" Julia asked. "I know this wasn't exactly what you planned."

"I'm okay with it," Alice admitted. "Truth is, I'm about tired of my house. It's got some issues."

"A few," Julia agreed with a smirk.

"I'm just tired of sinking money into it. And besides, if my dad walks on the practice I may as well start looking for a place in Sheffield any way."

"He's planning on retiring?"

"Yep. At the end of the year, so he says, but I have a feeling it will be sooner."

"So that's why you called me," Julia realized.

"I was feeling a little... overwhelmed. I mean, I already take most of the calls any way, but he runs the office and takes care of local pets and the like. We're a team. I'd have to find someone to replace him. And not to mention a secretary or something because the one we have isn't dependable. And a bookkeeper, because he does all that too. Just not sure if I want to run the practice."

"Seems like he has full confidence in you if he's already told you his plans of retiring and expecting you to take the reins."

"Oh, he's all about me running the place, I'm just the one questioning it. I mean, look at my life, Julia. I'm here, there, and everywhere. I sleep in barns. I haven't bathed in two days."

"*Two?!*" Julia tampered down her reaction when Alice flashed an "I-know-its-gross" look her way.

"I'm not an organized person," Alice admitted. "Like, at all. Having him anchor the clinic while I'm out and about just works. I can't imagine it not being like that."

"Well, you have some time. It's only June. Plenty of time to find some help."

"It's not easy around here, though. I mean, who wants to live in Sheffield? Or Parks? Or any of the other itty-bitty towns around here? Not many people."

"I think you need to stop stressing about it for now. The right person will come along." Julia walked towards the pantry. "He even bought cookies? That's it, I'm in love." She grabbed the box of chocolate chip cookies and opened them, offering one to Alice before taking a bite of her own. "Guess I could have stopped by the grocery store."

"You can do it tomorrow if you want. I'll be in Sheffield most of the day. You're welcome to come with me. Check out the clinic, see dad, get groceries, and then we can head back here in the evening. I'm grounded at the clinic tomorrow, so I won't be driving all over the place."

"Sounds like a plan. Now, if you will excuse me. I think I'm going to indulge in the bath facilities and then take a long nap."

"Go for it. I'm going to work the garden a bit and then I won't be far behind you."

Julia clasped a hand to her forehead. "I forgot about the garden."

"No worries. Looked like Seth was about done. I'm seriously just walking over there to see if I can steal some squash and zucchini."

Julia grinned. "Alright. See you in a few hours." She disappeared in her room, shutting the door and breathing in the scent of fresh laundered sheets, fresh picked flowers, and fresh air that only came from being out in the country. When she walked into the bathroom and spotted the oversized garden tub with fresh flowers and ivy spilling over the window ledge behind it, and candles staggered around it, she thanked God for this small slice of heaven. She also thanked Graham.

H

Chapter Six

Evenings on the ranch were one of his favorite sights to see. The sunsets full of vibrant reds, oranges, purples, and pinks always amazed him. Like snowflakes in winter, each had their own special design, no two ever the same. It was also one of the reasons he loved to walk the grounds one last time before calling it a day. He'd checked the horses, and all were fine with their oats and freshly cleaned stalls. Hayes saw to that. The garden was freshly picked and packed thanks to Seth. Lawrence had ordered feed. Clint helped Calvin finish clearing the fence line in the east pasture, and all the cattle were out to pasture thanks to the entire team of brothers. Now Graham navigated his way towards the chicken coop. He wasn't sure if Annie had checked on the hens or not when she buzzed in earlier in the day. He'd had quite a list for the faithful woman to knock out before Julia and Alice arrived, that he wasn't sure if she'd remembered to gather eggs. He circled around the back of the guest house towards the hen house, the evening breeze affording a nice reprieve from the day's heat. The small wooden and wired hut housed fifteen chickens that on a good day would provide him with eleven to a dozen eggs. He and his brothers were hardly ever without eggs. Though the rest of their kitchens may be empty, eggs were always available. He reached for a basket by the door.

"Are you collecting eggs?" Julia's voice drifted over to him and he spotted her sitting upon the railing of the small back porch of the guest house, her legs outstretched and crossed at the ankles. She held a cup of iced tea in her hands. She looked rested and at ease, and if he were being honest with himself, too pretty sitting that way.

"I am."

"Mind if I join you? I've always wanted to do that."

She didn't wait for an answer, but swung her legs to the ground and set her cup on the railing. She bounded down the two steps towards him. "How was your day?" She smiled as she slipped the basket from his grasp and draped it over her elbow.

"Good." He opened the coop door and ducked inside. He had to remain hunched over so as to fit in the small hut, but Julia was able to stand with only a slight tilt of her head to avoid the ceiling.

"So you just pluck them out of the nests?"

"That's the idea," he said.

"Simple enough." She smiled and walked over to the first nest and picked the egg up and gently placed it in the basket. "It's like an Easter egg hunt." She squatted to reach behind the row of nests. "Looks like there's a couple back here."

"Careful," Graham warned. "Check for snakes."

She retreated her hand quickly. "Snakes?"

"Not saying there is one, just have to be watchful."

"Well, Philip failed to mention that," she mumbled, reaching back behind the nests to retrieve the two eggs.

"Philip?"

"Your brother."

Graham crossed his arms. "I know my brother, yes."

"He warned me of creatures I needed to look out for. He didn't mention snakes." She moved on to the next nests and plucked the eggs from each basket, a small smile lighting up her face at each one. She surveyed each egg before placing it in the basket.

"What all did he warn you about?" Graham asked.

"Well, he gave me skunk spray." She held up the basket. "This all of them?"

Graham eyed the few laying spots that now and again would hide hidden eggs. Not seeing anymore, he nodded.

"And of course, 'possums," Julia continued. "And... bears." She eyed him with a smirk.

"Bears?" Puzzled, he looked down at her as she softly chuckled and stepped out of the hen house. "There aren't any bears around here," he assured her.

"Not of the animal sort, I know."

Understanding dawned on his face. "Ah."

She grinned and he forced himself to stay stoic. "You think I'm a bear?"

"Not my words. Your brother's," she clarified. "I was just an innocent bystander." She held the basket out to him.

"Need any?" he asked.

"I don't think so. I believe there was a small carton in the fridge. Plus, I'm going to Sheffield tomorrow with Alice, so I will pick up whatever else we'll need there. Thank you, by the way, for stocking some essentials. Especially the cookies."

"Gotta have a sweet in the house."

"I agree." She beamed up at him as he started to walk towards the main house. "What do you do with the eggs now?"

"I eat them." His brow furrowed as if she should know that.

"I meant, do you cart them up? Do you give some to your brothers?"

"Ah." He motioned her inside and to the mudroom on the side of the house. A separate refrigerator was plugged in and a counter with empty egg cartons sat to the left of it. He placed the basket on the counter and began filling a carton. "Eggs get carted, dated, and then placed in here. If anyone needs eggs, they come get them here." He opened the fridge and slid the carton in amongst several others. "Everyone takes the oldest batch first to use them up before these will get used. Feel free to grab whatever you need while you're here."

"Thanks."

He closed the refrigerator and continued on his way into the house, Julia still following behind him. He stopped and she waited patiently. "Did you need something else?" he asked.

Surprised, she nervously swiped a hand over her hair and backed up a step. "Oh, no. I'm good." She forced an embarrassed smile. "It's just...

Alice is asleep, and I took a nap earlier, so I'm a bit restless."

He said nothing.

"And..." she continued. "I thought maybe I could hang out with you."

"Me?" he asked.

"Sure. If you want." Taking his silence as rejection, her face turned crimson. "You know, you've probably had a long day and here I am chatting your ear off. I'll just go back to the guest house."

"We could go for a ride," he offered.

Her eyes sparkled at the idea as she nodded. "That would be great. I'd love to see more of the place."

He pointed to his truck. "Give me a second, and we'll head out."

She nodded and walked towards the truck. He hustled to the kitchen and grabbed his after-work beer that was thankfully restocked thanks to Annie. Hesitating a moment, he grabbed another one for Julia. He wasn't sure she even drank beer, considering she had a fruity drink at Sloppy's the night before, but he'd offer. It was the polite thing to do.

He climbed into his truck and handed her the bottle. She nibbled her lip to bite back a smile as she accepted it. He cranked the engine and rolled down the windows. "It's too much land to see in one trip, but I'll show you the main portion here, so you'll know where everyone is at if you need anything."

"Sounds good."

∞

Julia liked the small kindnesses she saw from Graham. Though his brothers called him a bear, it was clear that Graham deeply cared about those around him. And as they drove around the ranch, his love for the family property was evident with each story, each description, each plan he envisioned for the place. He referred to himself as a steward of the land, and she liked that he took that role seriously. He pointed to a brick house with nice trees and landscaping surrounding it, and a large barn within walking distance. "That's Calvin's place," he explained.

"So you each have a house?"

"All but Seth. He lives with Lawrence right now while his house is still in the planning stages."

"I'm impressed you all get along enough to live in the same place."

He smirked. "Well, we may live in the same place, but we can't live in the same house."

She grinned at that and pointed to another house on the horizon. "Who lives there?"

"That's Hayes' place. He likes his privacy, so he's the farthest away from the main gate."

He circled around a large pasture, cows and calves sprinkled amongst the grass as far as the eye could see.

"These the calves you guys worked yesterday?"

"Yep."

"What happens to them now?"

"We'll keep them for about 4-6 months, wean them, graze them, and then sell them."

"And then the cycle starts all over again?" Julia asked.

"Pretty much. This is just half the herd. The other half will be our fall calving herd."

"There's so many."

"Yeah we had a good number this go around."

Julia studied him as he eased the pickup truck along the dirt road, his eyes surveying the herd. He leaned forward a bit, his hand reaching silently to the rifle tucked between the center console and Julia's seat. "What are you doing?" she whispered.

He shifted into park and eased his door open and stepped out. Quietly he rested the barrel of the gun on the windowsill aiming at something she couldn't see. "Graham," she whispered.

He held a hand up for her to be quiet. She watched as he took aim, his sight narrowed on his target. His shot rang out, just a few of the calves skittering from the noise. He stood, retrieved his rifle from the window and tucked it back into the truck. Climbing back into the truck, he rerouted the truck back towards the guest house. "Coyote," he said.

Julia placed a hand on her rapid heart. "Did you get him?"

"Yep."

Impressed, she wondered how he remained so calm after mastering such a shot. She hadn't even seen the animal until the bullet hit and it jumped. If that was even what she saw. It happened so quickly she wasn't sure.

"We should head back to the house. Sun's about to go, and I'm starving."

"Right. Good idea. Especially if coyotes are starting to come out and prowl. Yet another animal Philip did not mention."

"We try to stay on top of predators, especially around the calves." He reached for his beer and finished the last sip. He noticed Julia's bottle was empty as well and liked that she didn't seem picky.

He pulled up to the main house, where Alice sat waiting on the front steps, a mug in her hands.

"Out for a joy ride?"

"Alice, it was amazing." Julia jumped out of the truck and darted towards the porch, Graham taking his time.

"Really?" Alice's skepticism had Julia laughing.

Julia's hands flew as she began retelling their journey and Graham's shooting ability. "I mean, bam! Got him! I didn't even see the coyote! It was incredible!"

Graham leaned against the porch railing, Alice studying his pleased expression as he watched Julia share about their trip.

"Oh, and we collected eggs." She pointed. "Right back there."

"Well..." Alice grinned. "Sounds like you two had quite an adventure."

"How was your rest?" Julia asked.

"Splendid," Alice sighed, content as the orange cat sitting in her lap. She stroked its fur. "Curly and I were just waiting for either one of you to return so as to bum a meal off one of you."

Graham motioned for them to follow him inside the house, but Julia shook her head. "No. You've done plenty today. I'll do it."

His brows rose as well as Alice's.

"You'll do what?" Alice asked. "Cook?"

Julia crossed her arms. "I can cook," she assured them. "Besides, it's the least I can do." Hopeful, she looked to Graham. "You can go shower and change and by the time you're done, dinner will be almost finished."

"I think you underestimate the shortness of men's showers." Alice smirked up at Graham.

"Come on. Please? I'd like to." Her brown eyes bounced between the two of them.

"I don't care who cooks as long as I eat." Alice shrugged her shoulders, completely impartial.

"You can use my kitchen." Graham walked inside without further instruction and headed up the stairs.

Alice eyed him in wonder. "What did you do to him?"

"What do you mean?"

"That man has bent to your every request since you arrived in town."

"No he hasn't."

"Ummm... yes, he has," Alice pointed out. "He gave you a ride from Sloppy's. He helped you at my place. He let you stay at his guest house. He took you for a ride. He let you work with him. He's letting you use his kitchen. You've got the man under a spell. Graham is never this amiable."

"Amiable? You call hardly speaking amiable?"

"For Graham, yes." Alice laughed. "I'm sort of stunned."

"Well don't be. He barely talks. And I've only gotten him to smile once."

"So you're trying to get him to smile?" Alice asked curiously.

"Well, yeah." Julia rummaged through Graham's refrigerator and fished out a package of chicken breasts. She then walked to what she assumed was a pantry and was pleased to see a well-stocked selection of goods.

"Why?" Alice asked.

"Because he seems so serious all the time." Julia placed several cans on the counter and turned to navigate her way towards where she thought pots and pans might be located. Alice pointed a finger to the kitchen island and Julia bent and retrieved what she needed. She placed the cast iron skillet on the stove top and then preheated the oven. She turned several bottles beside the stove until she spotted the olive oil and drizzled it in the pan. "I don't think he has sun-dried tomatoes." Julia bit her bottom lip a moment before spotting a basket by the door full of vegetables that Seth no doubt left for his brother. She grabbed a couple of tomatoes and sliced them up, drizzled them with oil, and slid them into the oven.

"What are you doing?" Alice asked.

"I'm just roasting them a minute. Getting them a little more tender for my sauce," Julia explained.

Her hands worked quickly, the recipe a favorite and one she could easily remember. It was also delicious, which she hoped would show Graham and Alice that she could actually do something productive. For some reason, she felt they doubted she could. She seasoned the chicken breasts and placed them in the skillet, searing them on both sides and placed them on a plate next to the stove top. She then retrieved the tomatoes from the oven and set them aside as well. She heard footsteps on the stairs. "Already?"

"Told you. Men are quick."

Graham dirty and sweaty from a day's work was eye-catching. Graham freshly showered with damp hair curled around his neck with muscular arms showcased by the t-shirt he wore... Julia turned before drool began to drip from her mouth.

"I'm not done," she confessed. "But it won't be long."

He acknowledged her comment with a nod on his way to the fridge, fishing another beer out. He held it up towards Alice and she nodded, causing him to reach for another for himself. He walked to the pantry and emerged with a bottle of wine and stood next to Julia. "Would you like some of this?" he asked.

Her hands grew nervous at his nearness. The scent of his soap drifted over her and she focused intently on mincing the garlic.

"That sounds nice. Thanks."

He ignored Alice's chummy grin as he opened the bottle to let it breathe and walked to the cabinet to retrieve a wine glass. He handed Alice her beer and she toasted him before taking a long satisfying sip. He filled Julia's glass and set it next to her. "Need any help?"

"Nope. I got it." She glanced up and smiled and took just one guilty moment of pleasure and soaked in those navy blue eyes that stood so close to her. "You just... just relax at the table with Alice."

He walked towards the table, Julia taking a deep breath behind his back that had Alice biting back a laugh and receiving a scolding look from Julia.

H

Chapter Seven

"So, tomorrow is Sheffield, huh?" Graham asked Alice as they both waited patiently for the tantalizing dish Julia seemed to be whipping together in his kitchen with surprising skill. He had to admit, it was nice having someone cook for him. Not something he was used to, that was for sure. And she was rather pretty, fretting about his kitchen, nervous as a house fly.

"Yeah, Dad's a bit swamped with small pets. He needs me at home base to help catch up."

"Think you could run by Diamond X and pick up an order for me?"

"No, but Julia could." Alice beamed towards her friend, Julia completely unaware of their discussion as she stirred a sauce in the pan on the stove. She then placed the chicken in the skillet and covered it, sliding it into the oven. She tapped a timer on the microwave, and they watched as her shoulders visibly relaxed. She grabbed her glass of wine and turned towards the table, just then noticing they were watching her every move. The pretty flush that stained her cheeks at his perusal had his own pulse ticking a bit faster. There was definitely something brewing between them, he knew. He felt it. He would deny it, of course, but it was definitely there. It'd been a long time since he'd found a woman that interested him. Granted, most of his days were on the ranch. But he was a man, and a beautiful woman like Julia didn't stumble into their lives very often.

"You think you could grab something for Graham tomorrow while you're out and about in Sheffield?"

Julia nodded. "Sure." She smiled as she walked towards the table and took a vacant seat. "What is it?"

"Just some shirts and pants." Graham cleared his throat. "And some boots."

"Sure. I don't mind. I'll add it to my list. I plan to explore. Of course, after I offer my services at the vet clinic."

"And what would you do at the clinic?" Alice asked.

"Whatever you need help with. I can clean crates or pens, or restock supplies, or answer phones. I am free to help you with whatever."

"I might take you up on that for a few hours. Though I guarantee you will be missing museum work within the first half hour."

"Museum work?" Graham asked.

Julia smiled. "I manage a museum in Santa Fe, tours and such."

"More than that. She's at The Governor's Palace," Alice stated proudly. "Spiffy place."

"It does have some beautiful historical items," Julia agreed. Her buzzer dinged and she hopped to her feet. Wrapping her hand with a dish towel, she fished the skillet out of the oven and uncovered it. She fluffed a bowl of salad and plated three plates, followed by her chicken concoction and brought them to the table. When she sat, Alice extended a hand across the table towards Graham and grabbed one of Julia's, and Graham did the same. Surprise lit Julia's eyes and she stared at their joined hands a moment before meeting his gaze. He bowed his head and prayed thanks, lightly brushing his thumb over her knuckles as he said amen. Her hand was small and delicate in his own, and he reluctantly released it.

Alice groaned as she chewed her first bite. "This is incredible, Julia. I had no idea you could cook like this."

Julia beamed in pride. "Thanks. I like to cook."

"Well, you've officially made yourself the cook the entire time you're staying with me." Alice forked another bite into her mouth and closed her eyes. "That sauce…"

"Alright, do we need to leave you alone with the chicken?" Graham asked, slipping the first bite into his mouth. He froze as soon as the flavor hit his tongue and Alice nodded with a knowing smile.

"Rocks your world, doesn't it, Hastings?"

"Wow." Graham chewed and swallowed. "That's pretty incredible."

Julia took her own bite and seemed satisfied with her dish as well. "I'm glad you guys like it. It's always nerve-wracking cooking for other people."

"You can cook for me anytime." Alice lightly dabbed her napkin to her lips as a knock sounded on the door. Graham turned and spotted Calvin on the other side and waved him inside.

Cal's surprise was evident as he eyed their homey set up around the small dinette table. "Evening. Didn't mean to interrupt. Just wanted to hand off these." He fished some receipts out of his back pocket. "Fuel for the dozer," he explained to Graham.

"Come on in, Calvin." Julia stood and bustled over to the counter and began making another plate. "You haven't eaten, have you?" She was already walking a plate towards him. He glanced to Graham and his brother nodded.

"No, no I haven't. I just finished up."

"Bless your heart." She motioned towards the table and set his plate down before turning and retrieving one of Graham's beers from the fridge and walking it over to the table. Cal sat in stunned silence at being waited on and looked from Alice to Graham in question.

Alice wriggled her eyebrows and took another bite of her meal as Julia sat back down.

"I appreciate this, Julia. Thanks."

"No problem." Her smile radiated before she spotted Graham's frown. "What is it?"

He hadn't realized his annoyance flashed across his face. He wasn't annoyed so much having his brother interrupt their dinner, more that Julia supplied him with a beer. Why did that bother him? It wasn't that he couldn't buy more beer. He could share.

"Graham's having a hard time sharing his hidden treasure now that he's found it," Alice explained with a wink and laughed at Graham's expense.

She'd hit the nail on the head. He wasn't quite sure how he felt about Julia treating Calvin the same way she treated him.

"Oh, Alice" Julia waved away the comment and continued eating. "So Calvin or Cal?" she asked the brother.

"Either one. Though most people call me Cal."

"I like it." Julia took a sip of her wine. "I saw your house earlier."

His brow rose.

"You have a pretty spot."

"Thanks." Embarrassed by the extra attention, Cal rushed through his meal. Graham wasn't even sure his brother tasted a bite, he seemed so eager to retreat from Julia's presence. None of them were used to female attention it seemed and were out of practice with socializing.

"You finish up?" Graham asked.

Cal nodded. "Need to do some machinery maintenance and clean up tomorrow before starting on the next project."

Graham nodded.

"No shop-talk." Alice waved a hand towards the brothers.

"It's what we always do," Graham countered. "And you're just as bad."

"Well, not tonight. Tonight, I'm enjoying my amazing meal and drink, and don't even want to think about work of any kind. We should go dancin'."

Calvin guffawed. "What is happening right now?" He eyed Alice as if she were an alien from Roswell and Julia giggled as her friend held up her hands.

"I'm clean. I'm rested. I'm full. I'm as happy as a clam. Now, I want to do something fun."

"It's only Thursday night," Cal pointed out.

"So?"

"The closest dance hall is over sixty miles away, and not sure if they're even open on Thursdays. Besides, pretty sure no one will be there because again... it's *Thursday.*" Cal shook his head in bewilderment. "When was the last time you even went dancin'?"

Alice contemplated a moment. "Maybe five years ago."

Cal grinned and shook his head. "You're crazy sometimes, Al."

"Come on." She reached across the table and nudged everyone's hands. "It'd be fun."

"You have an early morning tomorrow," Julia reminded her. "And you would complain all day if you were tired."

"So?" Alice looked to Graham. "Come on Graham. When was the last time you let loose and boogied?"

Cal snorted as he finished his beer.

Graham turned his signature glare on his brother who seemed completely immune to its power.

"How about we think about it for the weekend?" Julia said. "Everyone's pretty tired after today."

"Not us. We napped." Alice clapped her hands. "We don't need them to go dancing. We're two young, and beautiful women. I imagine we'll have dance partners aplenty."

Graham didn't like the idea of Julia dancing with various men. The thought turned his face sour and Alice winked at him conspiratorially.

"I..." Julia looked like she'd rather wait to go dancing as well.

"Saturday," Graham stated. "We could probably do Saturday."

Cal's jaw dropped and Alice clapped her hands in success. "Doesn't help me tonight, but I'll take it!" She stood. "Now if you will excuse me, I'm going over to Cal's for a bit."

"You are?" Cal asked.

"Well, yeah. You just got finished with work, so I imagine you will shower and then be wide awake for a while. I need to burn some energy with someone who isn't winding down for the evening."

Cal stood. "Can't promise much of a good time." He stacked Alice's empty plate on his own and carried them to the sink. "I'm beat."

"Man, is everyone lame tonight?" Alice shook her head in disappointment but still began following the brother to the door. "We'll play cards or something." She patted Cal on the back in rapid succession as she nudged him onward.

"Thank you again, Julia, for the meal. It was fantastic. Graham." He nodded a farewell to his brother and accepted the shove to the middle of his back from Alice to push him out the door.

"Alice is going to find some sort of trouble to get into tonight." Julia gathered Graham's plate and her own and walked them over to the sink and began running the water.

"I'll get those," Graham stated.

"No. You won't." Julia pointed to his bandaged hand. "I've got them. Besides, I cooked."

"Exactly. The person who cooks shouldn't have to clean."

"I like that rule." She smiled. "But I don't want you to have to suffer through rebandaging your hand or the wrath of Alice."

He leaned his back against the counter and crossed his arms as he watched her wash dishes. He reached for her wine glass and topped it off and then fetched one for himself and did the same. When she was finished with the other dishes, he handed her the full glass.

"Come with me." He led the way to the front porch and motioned towards a rocking chair. He took the other. Curly the cat circled around his ankles before doing the same to Julia. "I appreciate the meal, Julia."

"Honestly, it's the least I can do. You've helped me out so much. And given me a luxurious place to stay."

"It's not that luxurious."

"Compared to Alice's..."

They both chuckled.

"I suppose it is," he agreed.

"Really, Graham, thank you. I know I'm a stranger, but you've welcomed me on the ranch anyway. And I appreciate that. I promise to also stay out of your hair."

"Not a big deal." He took a sip of wine. Not his favorite drink of choice, but he wanted to prolong his evening with Julia and if suffering through a glass of wine was the ticket, so be it. "So, do you like dancing?"

"Not at all." She laughed as he did. "But seems I have no choice."

"We still have a couple days. Maybe Alice will change her mind, or maybe we could come up with a better option."

"Like what? What all is there to do around here?"

He scratched his temple. "Well... there's a bowling alley in Sheffield."

"Bowling could be fun," she admitted. "I will admit I have not bowled since college."

"Yeah, it's been awhile for me too. There's a movie theatre as well, though I have zero clue as to what movies are showing."

"I doubt Alice would want to sit still that long. Sounds like bowling and maybe a meal are our potential tickets out of dancing."

Graham nodded, though the thought of holding Julia close on a dance floor didn't seem all that bad of an idea. He stowed that vision away as quickly as it'd come.

A truck pulled down the main road, a dust cloud following along behind it. "Hayes," Graham said. He waved, and the brother slowed to a stop on the curve out front of the main house. Graham stood. "Be right back." He walked over to his brother.

"What you got there, Graham?" Hayes grinned, his voice low as Graham approached his truck window.

"Company. Julia and Alice are staying at the guest house."

"That so?" Hayes didn't remark on the oddity, he just moved right along. One of the attributes Graham liked best about his brother.

"You seen Clint?"

"He's out this evenin'. Something about feeling antsy."

"That will be a nightmare tomorrow. If he's late in the mornin' we're going to have a sit down."

"He did fine this mornin', a little sluggish at first, but he came to around nine." Hayes glanced over Graham's shoulder towards the house. "I like her."

Graham didn't turn around, but placed his free hand in his pocket. "She's not too bad."

"You like her?"

"Well enough." Graham said.

"No, I mean *like* her," Hayes clarified.

"Am I in eighth grade?" Graham rolled his eyes.

"Just wonderin', geez. She's here for a couple weeks. Lots could happen with her livin' that close."

"Not even on my mind," Graham lied.

"Right. Well, it's on everybody else's." Hayes chuckled. "First pretty woman we've seen in a while has us all vying for her attention."

"And everyone will treat her with respect," Graham growled.

"Right. *Like.*" Hayes grinned and playfully punched Graham in the shoulder. "I'll take the hint, brother. She's not my type anyway." He laughed as he started to pull away and head home, leaving Graham frustrated that his views on Julia were that obvious to his brothers. He'd need to work on that. The last thing he needed was for Julia to know he was attracted to her. She was here for two weeks. Two weeks and she'd be gone. Yes, he'd just keep reminding himself of that.

"Julia, you remember my dad, Hank?" Alice motioned to the white-haired man behind the check-in counter, his lab coat starched, freshly pressed, and at least one size too big. His fluffy mustache wiggled when he spoke.

"Hi there, Julia. It's been a long time." He shook her hand. "How's New Mexico treating you?"

"Great, thank you." She eyed the stack of charts on the top of the counter and the supplies cart pushed to the side that was loaded down with wraps, leashes, vials, and bags of various chews. Four customers with pets sat in the small waiting area.

"We've got a busy morning." Hank grabbed a chart. "Vicki is out sick... again."

"Gotta fire her dad." Alice grabbed the next chart off the stack.

"I would if she were ever here." He chuckled as he called out, "Bean." A man with an English bulldog walked towards him. Hank brushed a hand over the dog's head. "Hi, Bean. Come on back."

Alice glanced at her chart and then to Julia. "Feel free to sneak out whenever you want. Looks like he's got a packed day."

Julia nodded as Alice called out, "Zeus." A German Shepherd was herded her way and directed down the hall. Julia slid behind the counter as the phone rang. She sat awkwardly a moment, not sure if she should answer it, or just go ahead and leave. After the second ring, she opted for answering.

"Sheffield Veterinary Clinic." Julia flipped through the calendar on the desk. "Looks like there is an opening Monday morning at ten. No ma'am, they are completely full today, unless it is an emergency. Okay, I will mark you down for ten. Take care." She penciled in the appointment. She then explored the secretary's area and realized the entire place was unorganized. *Vicki should be fired*, she thought. She immediately set to work righting the small space.

Alice walked out of the room and handed Julia the chart for Zeus. "You can just stack it somewhere and I'll put it away at the end of the day." She stopped as she saw what Julia was doing. "Can't help yourself, can you?"

"Sorry." Julia grimaced. "I can help. I told you I could. Also, I made an appointment for a Mrs. Graves and her cat, Snickers, Monday at ten."

Alice nodded. "Just don't make any appointments after four. That way if we run behind, we aren't here until seven or so."

"Got it."

Alice slipped behind the counter and showed Julia the checkout process as she checked Zeus and his owner. When they left, she grabbed the next chart. "And off I go again."

Julia smiled as she stood and walked Zeus' file over to a cabinet labeled "patients." Sure enough, this was the filing system. She slipped it back in its place. She then walked over to the supply cart and spotted the supply cabinets and shelves in a small room and wheeled the cart inside and began placing items corresponding with the correct label. It wasn't rocket science, but she liked to organize. And hopefully this would help Alice and Hank not to feel so overwhelmed.

By noon, Julia had scheduled eight appointments, checked out over twenty patient/pet combos, organized the desk area and supply closet, and cleaned the break room. Her stomach grumbled as Alice emerged with another patient. Julia smiled and accepted the chart.

"I'm starving," Alice said.

"I thought about sneaking out to grab some lunch," Julia said. "I can bring some back here."

"Sounds good." Alice sighed, and grabbed the next chart. Life in the office was not her favorite job in the world, but Julia felt it suited her just as much as sleeping in barns or working calves.

When Julia stepped outside, she breathed in a breath of fresh, non-pet-smelling air and climbed into her car. She'd googled restaurants earlier when she had a few minutes downtime and realized that barbecue sounded good. Which meant, she shuddered, the shredded tire parking lot was where she was headed. She drove down the street and spotted Diamond X, Graham's store and quickly pulled into a parking space. While she was at it, she might as well grab his order so she wouldn't forget, or worse, not have time later. She'd been more involved and busier at the clinic than she thought she'd be. And she actually liked it. All the adorable pets coming in and the hopefulness of their owners for Alice and Hank to heal them.

She opened the door, a loud cowbell ringing as she stepped inside to the smells of leather and boot polish. A young woman stood behind the counter dressed in full rodeo attire, complete with teased hair, bright fuchsia lipstick, and bedazzled belt buckle. "Hi there," she greeted. "What can I do for ya?"

"I'm here to pick up an order for a friend." Julia rested her purse on the counter.

"Name?"

"Graham Hastings."

The girl's brows rose. "I'll have to call and verify. What's your name?"

"Julia." She nodded permission to do what needed to be done and watched as the girl's blood-red nails typed on the computer. Having pulled up Graham's information she reached for the phone and dialed. "Hi there, Mr. Hastings. This is Becky over at Diamond X. We have a woman here to pick up your latest order, and I just wanted to verify." Her Texas twang carried a touch of flirtation as she cradled the phone between her shoulder and ear as she continued typing something into the computer. "I sure will, Mr. Hastings, you have a good day." She hung up. "He asked me to have you call him when you leave." She chuckled. "I'll just slip to the back and grab his things. You just wait your pretty little self right there." She bustled away and Julia wondered why Graham wished to speak with her. He knew she was to pick up his supplies. Becky returned and placed two bags on the counter. "Here ya are. Receipt is in the bag. It was charged to the card on file. If Mr. Hastings has any issues or wants to return, you just make sure he has his receipt, alright?" She winked at Julia. "Have a good day."

Julia thanked her and headed to her car, slipping the bags into the trunk. She then fished around in her cupholder for the old receipt with Graham's phone number scribbled on it. Finding it, she dialed his number.

His voice, deep and rich and holding that familiar edge of annoyance answered after the first ring. "This is Graham."

"Hey, Graham, it's Julia."

His tone changed from formal to more relaxed, but the edge was still there. Still Graham. "Just wanted to make sure they got everything I ordered in the bags."

"Yes. I checked to make sure."

"Thanks."

Silence hung between them.

"Was that all?" Julia asked.

He cleared his throat. "Um, yeah. Yes. That was it."

"Alright." She smiled at his awkwardness. "I want you to know I'm headed to go pick up barbecue."

"That so?"

"Yes. Even going to park my car in that dreadful parking lot. Aren't you proud of me?"

"So proud." She heard what appeared to be a smile in his voice and tried to envision his face.

"Anyways, I'll let you get back to work."

"Alice keepin' you busy?"

She bit back a smile as he carried on the conversation. "Yes. Well, she didn't ask me to do anything, but I've sort of taken it upon myself to do things around the clinic. I'm quite a good secretary, it would seem. Oh, and there was this super cute puppy that came in this morning. It was a mutt, but oh my goodness, Graham, he had the longest ears. So cute." Realizing she'd started to babble, she took a breath. "Sorry, it's just been fun. This is my first venture outside of the clinic since this morning."

"I'm glad you're having a good time."

"What have you been working on today?" she asked.

"Just work."

His simple reply had her rolling her eyes. "Right. Well, I will let you get back at it then. I've got to get lunch and then head back to the clinic."

"Listen," Graham interrupted. "If you don't have time to do your grocery shopping today..." He was quiet a moment and she could hear the sound of the wind blowing through his phone. "You're more than welcome to eat dinner at my place again."

Her heart fluttered.

"And Alice, of course."

"Of course," she quickly agreed. "Thanks. We'll see how the rest of the day goes."

"Right. Well, take care Julia."

"You too." She hung up and did a small dance in her chair, not realizing Becky from Diamond X was stepping out of the building headed to lunch. She grinned at Julia's display, no doubt putting two and two together. Embarrassed, Julia offered up a quick wave and backed out of the parking lot.

H

Chapter Eight

"Graham, if you needed my help, you should have asked me five hours ago." Annie placed her hands on her hips. Despite her delicate frame, Annie faced off against Hastings family members with equal stubbornness. Sometimes severe stubbornness displayed on a daily basis. She knew each and every brother like they were her own sons. And she'd withstood many a Graham glare without fear.

"I didn't think I'd be feeding them again," he explained.

"And why are you, may I ask?" She cocked her head to the side and watched as he rummaged through his pantry. "Especially after you had me stock the guest house with supplies. They're grown women, they can feed themselves."

Graham sighed. "I offered."

"I see." She crossed her arms. "Honey, if you're sweet on this Julia woman, just ask her out."

Graham's head snapped around. "I'm not sweet on anyone, Annie. I'm trying to be hospitable."

"Oh, hogwash. I haven't seen you this jumpy or grumpy since Molly Davis at junior prom." She chuckled and eased her hip against the door as she continued to watch him in motherly affection. "She must be pretty special if she's got you acting so out of character."

"Why is it so shocking to everyone that I am a nice person?" he asked.

"You are nice, sweetie. On the inside. It's your outside that looks like you chew gravel most of the time." She pointed to his scowl. "If you eased up on that jaw of yours from time to time and let that handsome smile out, I imagine you'd have plenty of women coming to call."

"I'm not after a woman."

The sound of Alice's truck pulling up next to his outside the house, followed by Julia's little red Honda had him glancing out the window.

"Oh look, they're here." Annie beamed as she crossed over to the screen door and waved. "Hey girls, over here."

Alice nodded in acknowledgment as Julia unloaded a few bags of groceries into the guest house. "Looks like they bought groceries," Annie reported to Graham. "You may be off the hook." She grinned at the disappointment that flashed across Graham's face. She patted his cheek and he frowned at her. "Oh, stop it." She chuckled as she turned back to the door. "Ya'll hungry?" she called out to Alice. "Graham and I were just discussing what to make for dinner."

Julia emerged from the guest house and walked towards Alice at the base of the porch. "She is pretty," Annie whispered to Graham and lightly nudged him with her elbow. Annie opened the screen door and let both women inside.

"Hi there. You must be Julia." Annie extended her hand. "I'm Annie."

Julia shook her hand and greeted her warmly. "I've heard a lot about you."

"And I you." Annie grinned. "Come on now, ladies, let's fix us a glass of wine and make Graham cook for us."

"Oh," Julia looked to Graham. "I forgot to call you. I was able to buy some groceries."

"So?" Alice said. "Bring them over here. We got the fixings for fajitas. If you want to fire up the grill, you can do your part."

Annie clapped her hands. "Fajitas sound perfect. Don't they, Graham?" She narrowed her eyes at him, and they silently exchanged a conversation that had him nodding. "Sure. If that's what you guys would like."

"It is," Alice confirmed. "I've been thinking about them the entire way over from Sheffield. How you been, Annie? Haven't seen you in a while." Alice accepted the generously poured wine glass from the white-haired woman and both made their way to the table. "I'm good. Henry is at Bingo tonight, so I'm here bugging the britches off of Graham. Julia, honey, I set your glass on the counter. I figured you and Graham would want to grab those groceries and bring them over."

"Of course, yes." Julia smiled and waited for Graham to shoot another warning look in Annie's direction before he followed her outside. "She seems nice." Julia led the way to the smaller house and opened the door. "I didn't put them away yet because I wasn't sure what the plan was for this evening." She began sorting through the bags and removing items that weren't needed and put them away.

"She is," Graham confirmed. "Most of the time. She can also give a whipping that'll make you sore for a week."

Julia grinned. "And I'm sure you hardly ever had a reason for a whipping growing up."

"Me? Never." He smirked. "Maybe two. I'm a fast learner."

She handed him a bag and grabbed one herself. "Oh, I also bought you this." She grabbed a case of his favorite beer. "Since you've been housing, feeding, and tolerating us, I figured it was the least I could do. Oh, and your Diamond X order is in my car. Here." She handed him the other grocery bag as they walked outside, and she hurried towards her trunk. She retrieved his bags and box of boots and carried them inside. "I'll just set them in here." She called over her shoulder as she walked to his living room and placed them on the couch.

Annie's brow rose.

"Graham needed an errand boy today," Alice explained.

"I hope you bought some new shirts. Some of yours are just sad," Annie scolded. "Not sure I have any extra fabric to keep mending holes."

"He did." Julia grabbed her glass of wine and joined the other two women at the table. "Buy shirts, I mean. I like the dark blue one," she told him. "It'll make your eyes pop."

Alice snorted as she swallowed a sip of wine and Annie looked pleased to see Julia's comment had Graham blushing.

"I'm sure that's why he bought it. Right, Graham?" Alice teased.

Not uttering a response, Graham started fishing ingredients out of the bags. "I'm going to start the grill." He disappeared outside.

Julia stood again and walked over to the bags. "I'll start on the sides."

"We can help," Annie offered and started to stand.

"Oh, no. Please, let me. As a thank you for setting up the guest house for us."

Annie liked the girl more and more. "I won't say no to that, Julia. Thank you. My feet are so sore today. I blame Lawrence, though I can't stay too mad at that sweet boy for too long."

"What'd he have you doing?" Alice asked.

"Oh, I was cleaning his house today. It's not so much him I should be nagging about, but Seth. That boy doesn't know how to clean up after himself. Lawrence is just too good of a soul to kick his own brother out. It's time Seth gets after it."

"He needs a good Annie scolding," Alice encouraged.

"Oh, he got one. Both of them, because Lawrence was standing right there. Though I pulled him aside and said for his sanity's sake and mine, he needed to help Seth get those house plans drawn up quick or else his house was going to suffer for it."

Julia walked over and placed a bowl of salsa, guacamole, and chips between the ladies and walked back to the counter to start working on rice.

"Now this speaks to my heart." Annie dipped her first chip in the roasted red salsa and ate. "I think that might just hit the spot. Elbows off the table, Alice." Alice obeyed and dipped her own chip. "Now, how's your daddy? And the clinic?" Annie asked.

"Good, and better now that Julia completely revamped the place today."

"Did she now?" Annie looked over to the brunette bustling around Graham's kitchen and liked what she saw. Graham walked back inside, and Julia intercepted him with a sheet pan full of meat and handed it to him. Without a word, he stepped back outside.

"Yes," Alice continued. "I'm sad she's only here a couple of weeks. I'd recruit her in a heartbeat."

"You only say that because I cleaned up the dog vomit this afternoon," Julia chimed in.

"That and behind the desk. Both were equally disgusting to me."

Annie chuckled. "The poor girl comes to visit you on her vacation, and you put her to work."

"I don't mind it much. I like to stay busy." Julia turned the rice on to boil, adding spices and flavors that fragranced the kitchen.

Graham stepped back inside, and Julia stepped towards him to grab the pan. He shook his head. "I got it. Keep doing what you're doing." He walked over to the sink and began washing the sheet pan with warm soapy water. He felt her eyes on him and he turned to see Annie studying him closely. He tried to send her a mental "knock it off" but Annie just grinned. His hope of seeming less obvious in his attraction to Julia seemed to be failing. He didn't think he was acting much differently, but apparently, he was. He turned and Julia gasped as she'd turned at the same time and her bowl of beans spilled down the front of his stomach and pants. He flinched as they both stood a moment, frozen in motion, both gauging their next move. The beans were hot, but not scalding, the sludge slopping to the floor. Her panicked brown eyes darted up to his. "

"I am so sorry." Julia nervously placed the bowl on the island and began swiping her hands down the front of his shirt to swipe away refried beans. Realizing her efforts were pointless, she took a cautious step back and held her hands to her sides. "Graham—" She started to apologize again, but he just shook his head.

"I'm going to change. Watch the meat." He disappeared up the stairs and Julia looked to the other women in horror.

"I feel so bad." She dropped to her knees and began swiping up her mess. "Ugh, I can be so clumsy."

"Honey, that boy wasn't looking where he was going either. It's fine." Annie stood and walked to the door. "I'll go flip the meat right quick. Alice," Annie snapped her fingers and pointed to the mess on the floor. "Help her clean this up. You can't just sit there and expect a free meal all the time." And with that, she walked outside.

∞

"I cannot believe I just spilled beans all down the front of Graham." Julia tossed the last of the ruined beans in the trash and walked to his pantry hoping he had a couple of cans of beans inside. Thankfully, he did. She retrieved them and placed them on the island as Alice washed her hands. "So smooth," Julia muttered. "He's already being so nice to let us eat over here and then I go and mess it up."

"Don't be so hard on yourself." Alice acknowledged Annie's return with a nod as she walked back to her seat at the table and they both watched Julia fret about the kitchen. "If anything, I bet he enjoyed you wiping your hands down the front of him."

Julia's mouth dropped. "I did no such thing." Her face flushed crimson. "Well, not in the way you mean. I was trying to clean the beans off of him."

"Were you?" Alice teased. "Get a good feel of his abs in the process?"

Annie chuckled as Julia's face flamed an even brighter shade of red. "I did not, thank you very much. That would have been—"

"Delightful?" Alice finished.

"No." Julia started to place her dirty hands on her hips and stopped realizing they were covered in beans and walked to the sink to rinse them off.

"Delicious," Annie added and made Alice laugh and Julia's lips twitch.

"No." Julia tried to keep a straight face as the women continued to tease her. Graham's footsteps had her holding a finger to her lips and giving the two women a warning look.

"Meat was almost done," Annie reported when his foot hit the last step. "Best take it off to rest. Looks like Julia's almost done with everything else. You soak that shirt?"

"It's in the laundry room."

"Yes, but are you soaking it?"

"Yes ma'am."

"Good man." Annie nodded in approval.

"Graham, again, I apologize." Julia reached towards him and lightly grazed her fingers over his arm, debating if she should reach out to him or not. Her hand fell to her side when his navy eyes landed on her. He didn't seem angry, which was a good sign, but his expression was unreadable.

"It's no big deal." He walked out to the porch to fetch the meat.

Julia blew a frustrated breath. "Guess that's all I'm going to get out of him."

"What did you expect?" Alice asked.

"I don't know." Julia shrugged.

"I think the real question is, what do you want to get out of him?" Annie asked. "That boy's always been the quiet, serious sort. It's his nature. Always watchful, protective, stubborn, and a bit stand-offish. Don't let that scare ya, honey."

"He doesn't scare me," Julia assured her. "He's just a hard one to get to know."

"And Julia *really* wants to get to know him," Alice baited.

"Hush." Julia slapped a towel her direction. "I do not. Well, I do. But I want to get to know all of the brothers."

"Oh, so should we be expectin' more company?" Annie glanced at her watch and Alice laughed.

Julia inhaled a deep breath and caved. "Okay, fine. I find him intriguing." She pointed a finger at the two women. "*Don't* say anything. Besides I'm only here a couple weeks, not like I can get to know him that well anyway. Just thought it would be nice to have some friends to talk and hang out with whenever you're busy the next couple weeks."

"So, you choose the most alienated man in Parks?" Alice pursed her lips as she nodded. "Good plan." Her sarcasm dripped like dark honey and had Annie chuckling.

"Oh, how I love that boy." Annie grinned. "Shake him up, Julia, even if it is for a couple of weeks. It's time he sees there is life outside this ranch."

Graham walked back inside and caught the last of Annie's sentence. "Life outside the ranch, what?"

"Nosey." Annie waved away his interruption. "Just telling Julia you boys needed a life outside the ranch."

"We're happy with the way things are," Graham grumbled, turning his back to them as he transferred the meat to a large cutting board and walked the pan over to the sink once more.

"Sure you are. So, you girls plan on church this Sunday?"

"I believe so," Alice said. Julia just nodded as if she were here for whatever Alice wanted.

"Good. You'll sit by us," Annie invited. "Sixth pew on the left."

"I know where you sit," Alice stated.

"Oh, do you? I hadn't seen your face there in a while, so I wasn't sure you remembered."

"I get it, Annie." Alice smiled. "I've been lazy in my attendance the last several months."

"If I can get all seven Hastings brothers to church every Sunday, then Alice Wilkenson, you can drag your butt there too. Besides, I've got pot roast planned for Sunday lunch at my place. Henry loves his company on Sundays."

"The boys confessed their lack of attendance lately," Alice pointed out. "But how is Henry?" Alice asked, concern etching her forehead.

"Oh, the same horse's behind he always is," Annie affectionately said. "That's my husband," she told Julia. "He and Graham are two peas in a pod."

"Because they're both horse behinds?" Alice asked with a smug grin towards Graham as he turned to let his dislike of her comment be known.

Julia patted him on the back as she reached for the shredded cheese beside him. "She only recognizes those of her own kind," Julia whispered and had his face lifting into that charming smile before he laughed at Alice and Annie's surprised faces. Julia wrinkled her nose and stuck out her tongue at Alice before continuing her task of setting out the sides on the island. She pivoted to check the rice on the stove and her shoe slipped in the damp spot on the floor where the beans had been cleaned. Graham caught her by the elbow before she landed hard against the island, and her heart bounced into overdrive.

"Karma," Alice whispered as she took a sip of her wine.

Julia placed a hand over her heart. "Thanks for the save. Guess I didn't wipe up the grease as well as I thought." His grip lingered on her arm as she looked up at him, and his face grew serious. Something shifted and stirred between them, like the wind before a storm, heavy and full of a potential outburst.

"Ahem." Alice broke the silence. "You'll have your chance to hold her close when we go dancing tomorrow night. Is the food ready?"

Julia jumped from his touch and began setting out the plates.

"Dancing?" Annie's eyebrows lifted and shook her shoulders. "That sounds fun."

"Actually, about that," Julia began.

"Already backing out?" Alice frowned.

"Well, Graham and I were talking, and we—"

"Were you now?" Alice crossed her arms and waited patiently for an excuse.

"We were thinking bowling instead," Julia rushed to finish as she handed a plate to Graham and Annie.

"Bowling?"

"Yes. And dinner, maybe."

Alice pondered the idea. "That could be fun. Alright, let's do it. I'll group text the rest of the family."

Julia sent a wink towards Graham at their success of changing the dancing plans. The exchange did not go unnoticed by Annie, but she didn't say a word other than to bow her head and wait for Graham to say grace. When he obliged, the rest of the evening was spent with Annie sharing embarrassing and sweet childhood stories of Graham and his brothers' shenanigans that only endeared Julia to them more. Annie's love for them was obvious, and Graham treated the woman like a mother. Their bond special, and she was glad that Annie hugged her before leaving and seemed to like her.

"She's absolutely wonderful," Julia stated as they all stood on the porch and waved a farewell as Annie headed home.

"We wouldn't have lived past the age of ten if it weren't for her and Henry," Graham acknowledged. "Seth especially. He was always up to mischief."

"Annie is definitely a gem. Well, the clinic is closed tomorrow, so I'll be around if you need me," Alice told Graham. "I'll walk the garden in the morning and then after that I'm yours for whatever work."

Graham nodded.

"And me too." Julia raised her hand. "I can help with something too. I have no idea what, but I'm willing to."

"You can ride with me," Graham said. "You can see some more of the place."

Julia's heart skipped at the invitation and when those navy blues looked at her, she felt her smile widen in response. She wasn't sure if it was her imagination, but she thought they looked softer than they usually did. Perhaps Graham was warming up to her after all.

H

Chapter Nine

He loved weekends on the ranch. Yes, there was still work that needed to be done, but the pace was slower. Restful. He'd sleep in, which typically meant to around seven, cook himself a good breakfast, enjoy his coffee on the porch, knock out any projects around the house, and then he'd drive around the ranch and check the progress of whatever work his brothers' worked on during the week. It was peaceful, soaking in the fresh dew, the sunrise, the beauty of the land. It also set his mind at ease to come up with a game plan for the next week before checking out completely for the rest of the weekend. He'd make a list, set it by the door and his work boots, and come Monday morning, bright and early, the work he loved would be waiting for him. On his way to his truck he loaded a bag of mineral. If he was to ride around and check on the cows, he might as well check the mineral and the water troughs while he was at it.

"Morning, Graham." Julia's voice drifted over to him. She sat on the front porch of the guest house, a cup of coffee in her hand, and fuzzy slippers on her feet.

"Mornin'."

He wasn't sure if he should walk over and talk to her, or if just going about his business was the right thing to do. She pardoned him with a simple, "Have a good morning."

"You too." He nodded in farewell as he climbed behind the wheel of his truck and set out towards the first pasture. Elbow draped over the open window, the cool breeze of the morning completed his morning wake up routine by crisply teasing his face. It would be another couple of hours before the heat of the day would start creeping up. He aimed to be finished by then. The summer sun was brutal in west Texas, temperatures climbing to over 100 degrees Fahrenheit without delay. Summers called for early mornings, long lunches inside out of the sun, and then once the heat of the day began to decrease, another round of work would proceed late into the evening or night. There were just some days it was too hot to be outside working. Thankfully, the routine of the ranch wasn't new to him or his brothers, and most of them were able to make those early mornings on time.

He reached the first water trough and also peeked into the mineral bin. Nothing more than an oversized tire cut in half and flipped inside out, it served as the perfect serving bowl for cattle. He hopped out, poured some mineral in the tire, peered into the water trough and though he felt it a little lower than he'd like, wasn't alarmed. It'd been a hot few days. Water levels would be somewhat low depending on how much water the cattle were consuming. He made a mental note to check water levels at *all* the water troughs to be sure. Clint hadn't mentioned low water levels, and it was Clint's responsibility to check the troughs every other day.

His cell phone rang, and Hayes requested his presence at the horse stalls. Mineral and troughs would have to wait. He redirected himself towards the stalls and pulled up in time to see their newest acquisition bucking his brother off the saddle and causing him to land hard in the dirt. An annoyed grunt and growl had Hayes pushing himself to his feet. "I hate 'im."

"He's still fresh. It'll take some time."

"Nope. I hate 'im. I don't say that about a lot of horses, but this one... he's hopeless. I know we got a good deal on him, but I just don't see him being a good workin' horse, Graham. He doesn't trust me. He doesn't trust Lawrence. And Lord help us if he even lays eyes on Clint. He has a hard enough time riding any way." He rubbed his backside, no doubt a sore tailbone from his fall. "I've been working him for about twenty minutes. I think that's it for this mornin'. I don't want to completely tick him off."

"That's fine." Graham watched as Hayes eased his way towards the horse and grabbed the reins. The horse tugged against his pull, but then fell into step once he realized he would receive a bucket of oats, a good brushing, and a low-key rest of the morning.

Hayes was great with horses. He was great with any animal, really. So for him to question their latest buy concerned Graham. They needed a couple of younger horses to be reliable enough to handle working cows. Graham loved his horse. But Trisket was aging out, and fast. She was eleven years old, not too bad for a horse. But they'd worked a lot of hours together, and he wanted his horse to have a relaxing retirement. Easy rides around the pastures, not working cattle.

Hayes emerged from the barn swiping his sleeve over his sweaty forehead. "What's the plan this mornin'?"

"Ridin'."

No other explanation was needed. Hayes knew Graham's routine.

"Thought I might head to Sheffield. I need some food in the house. Hadn't had time for much shoppin'."

"That's fine. As far as I know, not much of anything going on this morning. But I think we are expected to go bowling this evening."

"I heard about that." Hayes grinned and wriggled his eyebrows. "From what Al said, it was you and Julia who came up with that plan. *Together*."

"We both hate dancing. It was an easy alternative."

"Right." Hayes winked. "She sure is a pretty thing. And sweet too. Pretty sure I got a toothache just talkin' to her the other day."

Graham snorted as Hayes unapologetically smiled. "Too bad a woman like that wouldn't enjoy life out here."

"Why do you say that?"

"Look at her, Graham. That girl is all city from head to toe. I bet she uses fancy shampoo on that glossy hair of hers and her high heels probably cost more than a ton of feed."

His brother was probably right. However, Graham was more annoyed with himself for being disappointed at the obvious observation.

"But hey," Hayes slapped Graham's shoulder. "maybe she's got friends." He grinned. "I'm headed for a shower. See you this evening."

Hayes wandered to his truck and Graham sat a moment and watched the few horses in the pen circle about and graze. Maybe he should make a stop by the feed store and talk to Philip about upping the concentrates order for the horses. He'd call and see when Hayes last placed the order. Taking on a new horse meant an increase in food supply and he hadn't asked Hayes if he'd seen to that yet. He probably had. Hayes was detail oriented, but Graham still needed the peace of mind in the moment. He dialed Philip's number and his brother answered on the second ring. "It is Saturday, Graham. My day off. What's up?"

"Right, sorry. Just wanted to see if Hayes altered our horse concentrate numbers recently?"

"Yes. Last week."

"Good. Good deal."

"You could have asked Hayes," Philip yawned into the phone.

"He just left. I forgot. You were the next best thing."

"Glad I could help."

"So, not sure if Alice told you, but we're all going bowling tonight if you want to join."

"She mentioned it." Philip stretched and walked from his kitchen island over to his coffee pot for a second cup of coffee. "I'll aim to be there. Glad you guys are taking a night off."

"It happens every now and then."

"When a pretty face comes to town?" Philip chuckled. "I don't blame you. Clean up nice tonight, Graham."

"I should say the same to you."

"I'm not trying to impress Julia," Philip stated.

"And I am?"

"From what Al told me you aren't really having to. Seems Ms. Julia finds you fascinating as is. None of us get it, of course, but we all find it amusing."

"I don't know what you're talking about. I've been a hospitable host. That's it."

"Okay." Philip shrugged in indifference, the action reflecting in his tone on the other side of the line. "Whatever you say, big brother. See you later." He hung up before Graham could lay into him more.

"Brothers," he muttered under his breath, annoyed, once again, that everyone seemed to think he pined for Julia McComas. The last thing Graham Hastings did was pine for a woman. And a prissy one at that. But he liked the idea of Julia maybe taking a liking to him. *Was that wrong?*

Maybe it was. He was just never really the likable sort. Clint never had a hard time catching a lady's eye. And Philip seemed to be doing alright. Maybe it felt a little nice to be the brother to catch this particular woman's eye. It was certainly a new feeling, but thinking about Julia on the front porch this morning, he realized he kind of liked the feeling. And that bugged him too.

∞

"You should just plant one on him." Alice walked from her bedroom to the cozy living room rubbing a towel through her damp blonde hair. She sat in the chair opposite Julia. "A big smooch that knocks his socks off."

"I'm not going to kiss a man I barely know." Julia rolled her eyes.

"Why not? It's obvious you two have something going on."

Julia scoffed. "I think I'm just distracted by a handsome face. I'm sure it's nothing. Tonight, when we're hanging out with the other brothers it will seem like nothing."

"You think so?" Alice shook her head. "I don't think so. Even from my view last night it was clear there was some electricity bouncing between you and Graham. Annie saw it too."

"I'm not here for romance." Julia tossed her magazine on the coffee table and then snuggled back into the chair with a blanket.

"There's nothing wrong with a little vacation romance."

"Alice, he's your friend. More like family with the way you act around these guys. I don't want to interfere with the relationship you guys have, nor come in and be a quick little fling. It's not my style. And I can tell it is not Graham's either."

"So, say it's not a fling." Alice held up her hand to pause Julia's interruption. "I mean, I wouldn't mind having my best friend close by."

Julia laughed. "Right, and what could I possibly do in Parks for work?"

"You could work at the clinic with me."

"Ah." Julia grinned. "Now I see where this is going."

Alice tossed her head back and forth as if jostling an idea loose. "It's not my only motive."

"Well, I'm glad I was able to help you yesterday. And it was fun. But I love Santa Fe. It's my home."

"Oh, but think of it Julia. You and Graham." Alice stood and walked her towel back to her bathroom. "He's all broody and handsome and you're like a ray of sunshine and beautiful. Match made in heaven." She walked back into the room and plopped back into her chair.

Julia pointed to the kitchen counter at a cup of coffee that she'd prepared and had cooling. Alice hopped back to her feet with a smile, grabbed the mug, and eased back into her chair. She took a satisfying sip. "Just how I like it."

"I don't think Graham is interested in anything other than this ranch."

"Oh, he's interested in more than that," Alice mumbled as she sipped her coffee. "Whether or not he'll act on it is the question. You've got to give stronger signals."

"Me?" Julia looked dumbfounded. "Again, I'm not looking for anything from him or anyone. And if he is interested or wants to get to know me better then he better start talking. He barely says a word, Alice. How is anyone supposed to get to know him when he's so closed off."

"He's just got a lot on his plate. And he's a bit rusty when it comes to socializing with the human race outside of his family," Alice defended.

"And? You want me to start seeing a man who barely speaks to me all because he's shy, busy, or has too much responsibility and is too proud to share any of it with his brothers? This already sounds like it is off to a successful start." Julia rolled her eyes and stood to walk to the coffee pot for a second cup of coffee. "I will admit, I find him attractive. A woman would have to be blind not to. All the brothers are good looking. And he seems like a nice man underneath that glower of his, but that's not enough to turn my head at this point."

"What would be enough?" Alice asked. "In the years I've known you, you've only had two serious relationships. And even then, they both only lasted a year."

"I'm picky." Julia walked back over and sat. "Nothing wrong with that. And I could easily toss that back at you, Ms. I'm-too-busy-because-I-birth-horses-and-sleep-in-barns."

"Hey, I have my fun. I go on dates here and there. Just because I haven't found a serious relationship doesn't mean I've closed myself off to the opportunity of having one."

The crunch of gravel had both women glancing out the front window to see Lawrence, Seth, and Sloppy emerge from Lawrence's truck.

"Wonder what they're up to." Alice walked to the front door, opened it, and yelled. "What are you ruffians doing today? It's a little early for shenanigans, isn't it?"

Ruby smiled and darted over to the porch. "We're going to ride horses this morning."

She waved towards Julia inside the house as she walked out onto the porch. Lawrence tipped his hat towards them on his way into Graham's as Seth walked up and draped his arm over Ruby's shoulders. She shrugged him off and unoffended, he leaned against the porch post. "Mornin' ladies." He grinned.

"Morning."

"We're here to raid Graham's coffee on the way to the stalls."

"He left hours ago," Julia said. "There may not be any. If there's not, we still have some."

"Much obliged, Jewels. Can I call ya Jewels?" he asked, slipping by them and into the guest house. Lawrence emerged from Graham's house with a shake of his head.

"Why does everyone raid Graham's coffee?" Julia asked.

"It's the best." Seth poured the remainder of the pot into his thermos. "He buys that fancy stuff online."

Julia's brow arched in surprise.

"Yeah, has it shipped in," Lawrence added. "Not sure where he came across it, but Graham's a coffee snob."

"Why don't you guys just order yourself some?" Julia asked.

"And not annoy him?" Seth shook his head. "No. It's better this way." He grinned.

"You guys are getting a bit of a late start this morning." Alice glanced at the clock. "It's almost ten."

"It's Saturday," Seth replied. "Not all of us wake up at the crack of dawn on Saturday."

"Only when we need to." Lawrence set about brewing another pot of coffee. He took Ruby's thermos and set it on the counter by his. "Besides, I woke up early to go pick up Slop."

Julia noticed the slight cringe from Ruby at him using her nickname.

"Do you come out here often, Ruby?" Julia asked.

"Every now and then when the brother's have time to deal with my amateur abilities in the saddle."

"You're getting better," Lawrence encouraged. "Takes practice."

"You're better than I would be." Julia smiled. "I've never ridden a horse before, so I'm sure you're leaps and bounds ahead of me."

"Never ridden a horse?" Seth draped his arm over Julia's shoulders and squeezed. "We need to remedy that. Suit up, Jewels, I'll take ya for a spin."

"Um no." Alice removed his arm from her friend's shoulders. "Julia and I have a full day planned."

"We do?" Julia asked and then slowly nodded as Alice widened her eyes her direction and bobbed her head up and down real slow. "Ah, yes, we do," Julia agreed. "Super busy."

"Well, maybe another time." Seth winked. "Come on, Lawrence."

Lawrence finished filling his and Ruby's thermoses and walked towards the door. "Thanks for letting us bum some brew."

"Anytime." Julia smiled and waved as they all left.

"So why did you not want me riding with Seth?"

"Of all brothers in the saddle, Seth has had the most accidents."

"Gotcha. Thanks for the save, then."

"Don't mention it. Besides, he was making googly eyes at you."

Julia laughed. "He was not."

"You're female, *Jewels*," she stressed the nickname. "Seth was definitely making googly eyes."

"He's too young for me."

"Age is but a number," Alice chuckled. "And Seth isn't good at math."

Laughing, Julia and Alice split their separate directions to head to their bedrooms and change into their clothes for the day. Julia, despite realizing Seth was young, enjoyed the pep to her step that only came from a man's complimentary attention. Though she reminded herself to be cautious around Seth so as not to encourage more of it. Graham, on the other hand, she wondered what would gain more of his consideration. Now that was a question for the ages, she thought.

H

Chapter Ten

The women were out and about somewhere when he'd darted home for lunch. Which was fine. He'd been able to grab a brief nap in his favorite recliner without interruption. Rested and rejuvenated, he opted for finishing his mineral run and water trough checks. He loaded up the bed of his truck with more bags of mineral and he'd just made it as far as the western pasture when he came across a dry trough. He took a deep breath as his frustration towards Clint swelled inside his chest. He'd wait to hound his brother once he knew what the problem was. He stepped out of the truck and checked the float valve. It wasn't hung up. Maybe the valve was clogged and that was preventing the water from flowing. He took the valve apart. No clog. He leaned back on his haunches in the grass and looked up at the sky, praying for more patience.

He darted to his truck to go check the other troughs. If this one was dry, he prayed the others still had enough water. The next water trough was low. The farthest trough was only half full and absolutely no water pressure at any of them.

"This isn't good," he mumbled, as he realized no water pressure was coming up the line. He started tracing the line back to the 20,000 gallon stone pila. Maybe it was a clog at the pila. It was either that or the well was down that supplied the pila. Either way, the situation wasn't good. Reaching the pila, Graham noticed its low water level and lost his temper towards his brother. This could only happen if Clint had neglected to check the troughs the last few days. They only had enough water for a day, and it was too hot for the cows not to have an ample supply of water. He checked the solar pump well by the pila. He glanced at his watch again and realized it was now four o' clock. Didn't look like he'd be making that bowling night out. He dialed Alice's number.

"You gettin' spiffy yet?" she asked.

"Not quite. Look, I'm not going to make it."

"What?"

"Stumbled across a dry trough and I'm trying to figure out the problem."

Alice growled in frustration. "I'll tell you the problem, Clint's been going out and dilly-dallying instead of checking water levels."

"Exactly. But that's the least of my problems right now. May be a few of us missing out on tonight if I can't get this pump to working. I'm resetting the control box now to see if that does it."

"I pray it does. You call Cal?"

"Not yet. Going to see if this works first."

"Alright. Well, just keep me posted."

"Will do." He hung up, slipping his phone back into his pocket.

Pump Overload Failure. The screen reported.

"Great." He fished out his phone again and dialed Calvin.

"Hey bro." Cal's upbeat tone filled Graham with instant regret at interrupting what was to be one of their nights free of ranch responsibilities.

"Need your help pulling a pump."

"You're kidding, right?"

"Nope."

"Clint," Calvin muttered. "Fine. Where you at?"

"North Pasture."

"Sanded up again? Or have you tried a reset?"

"Sanded up. And yes. We're going to have to pull the pump."

"Not exactly how I planned to spend the evening."

"I already called Alice," Graham assured him.

Sighing, Cal continued. "I'll be out there in a bit with the rig." He hung up and Graham rubbed a hand over the back of his neck.

"A bit," was an hour and a half. Which, Graham conceded, was actually good timing on Cal's part. After all, Graham was in the farthest pasture from the main hub. And it meant his brother dropped whatever it was he had been doing and came as quickly as he could. Cal was good that way.

Cal stepped out and shut his truck door. "Well, are my hopes of you being wrong valid?"

"Nope."

"I was afraid of that. Alright, let's start pulling up pipe." He moved his truck into position, the wench on the front to be used to hoist the pipes up. Cal climbed up the windmill to connect to the pulley, while Graham hooked up the pipe in the well below.

The brothers worked in tandem and they successfully pulled the necessary 250 feet of pipe, removing the ten joints and setting the pipes aside. Graham's phone buzzed, but his hands were covered in mud. A text could wait.

"Um, Graham." Cal's dreaded tone had Graham walking over. "Got ourselves a frayed wire."

"You're kidding me?"

Cal shook his head.

"You got anything to splice it?"

"Not with me." Cal rubbed a hand over his weary face.

"Get Clint to bring what we need. It's his mess any way."

Cal dialed his brother while Graham checked his own phone. Alice.

A: "We opted for Sloppy's for dinner again instead. Julia didn't want to go bowling without you and Cal. If you guys wrap up the water situation, meet us there. Seven."

G: "Doubt we'll make it. We've had to pull pipe. Calling Clint to come out now to bring us an electrical box."

A: "Clint's here at the house. We've all been porch sitting."

That irked him. While he and Cal were wet and muddy the rest of his brothers were relaxing on a porch, drinking beers, entertaining Julia.

G: *"Get him here. Now."*

He knew Alice would convey his message on top of hearing Cal shouting into his phone. "It's your fault, you have to help. Get moving." Cal tossed his phone into his truck. "He's coming. Not sure how long he'll take."

"I've got Alice on his tail too."

"Good." Cal shook his head. "This is ridiculous." He spotted the bags of mineral in the back of Graham's truck. "Let me guess, he hasn't been putting that out either."

Graham groaned. He'd completely forgotten about the mineral in the midst of dealing with the troughs. "I started putting it out, but this distracted me."

"Sounds like it'd be a good job for Clint. Let's move the trucks before he gets here so we can shine some light on all this before it completely goes dark on us."

They rotated their trucks and faced their headlights on their work area. They sat on Cal's tailgate and waited. After an hour, Cal glanced at his watch. "Well, when do we just wash our hands of him and call someone else?"

At his words, headlights appeared and made their way towards them. Clint hopped out of the truck. "You two look like you've been mud wrestling."

"No thanks to you. Did you bring the electrical box?"

"Yep." Clint retrieved the tools and supplies needed to splice, seal, and waterproof the wires, Cal yanking it all from his hands and storming over towards the pump.

"Man, he's in a bit of a fit." Clint turned towards Graham and his eyes widened at the fury on his older brother's face.

"When's the last time you checked troughs?"

"A few days ago."

"When?" Graham challenged. Seeing how hard Clint had to think to remember told him everything he needed to know.

"I thought so. Congratulations, tomorrow you get to haul water to all the troughs so the cows have something to drink until the pump and pila catch up."

"Hey, I didn't—"

"Before sunrise," Graham continued. "For now, take the mineral bags out of my truck bed and put them in yours. I need you to finish putting out mineral tonight."

"I might as well do that in the morning when I'm checking troughs."

"I said do it now." Graham pointed to his truck and Clint, realizing it was obey or possibly die, did as he was told.

"Think I got it, Graham," Cal called. "Let's get this back down the hole."

Graham hurried over, tested the pump, and sighed in relief that it was working. "Alright, let's finish it up." He turned off the pump as they fitted the pipe back down the hole. An hour and a half later, Cal turned the pump on with a celebratory pump of his fist.

Clint's truck rolled back up and he rolled down the window. "Well?"

"It's working again. No thanks to you." Cal rubbed a handkerchief over his face.

"I'll say what I always say," Clint said. "This is why we need a redundant water source for each pasture."

Knowing the expense of such a request, he grinned at Graham.

"Or you could just check the water more frequently, like you're supposed to," Graham ordered.

"Yeah, enjoy your early morning." Cal stalked away from Clint's truck and began putting his tools away, Graham following close behind.

∞

She saw the flick of Graham's headlights as he pulled up to his house. Not that she'd been watching for him. Okay, she had been. Guiltily. Though she'd had a fun evening with the other brothers, he and Cal were missed. She hoped he saw her note on his screen door and realized she had him a meal keeping warm in the oven. It was the least she could do after he'd worked all day and into the night. She'd done the same for Cal, once Hayes agreed to drop it off on his way home. Clint, however, was on his own. She held a small grudge against him for slacking and making his brothers pick up that extra work. He had felt absolutely no remorse when he'd received the call from Cal. Alice reamed him a good one as well, but nothing seemed to phase him.

Tired, she set her book aside, not that she'd actually been reading it the last hour, but nonetheless, she sat it on her bedside table and turned off her lamp. In the morning she'd attend church with Alice and the Hastings, meeting Annie's husband, Henry, and the rest of the people of Parks. It would seem, from what Seth told her, that almost everyone in the small town made an attempt to attend on Sundays. She tossed and turned for another hour until finally, sleep came for her.

She woke up to the sound of a smoke alarm and bolted from the bed. Sprinting, she ran towards the kitchen and found Alice waving a dish towel beneath the alarm, a pan on the stove smoking and sizzling with burnt bacon.

"Blasted bacon burns every time!"

Julia ran to the windows and raised them up. "Why didn't you bake it?"

"Bake bacon?" Alice looked confused. "Didn't know that was a thing." She continued waving the towel as Julia pushed window after window and began fanning the front door. On her third swing, she almost slammed it right into Graham's face. She squealed at his sudden presence and held a hand to her heart as she waved him inside. "Alice was getting creative."

The alarm quieted and Alice tossed the hand towel onto the counter. "Phew, that one is a doozie."

"You woke up the whole ranch," Graham grumbled.

"Tell me about it." Julia shoved her tangled mass of hair over her shoulder and attempted to smooth her hands through it to look more presentable. She then realized she stood in a tank top and undies and nothing else. Gasping, she ran towards her bedroom to grab a pair of pants.

Alice laughed. "Get an eyeful?" she asked Graham.

"No." His annoyance with the alarm had him storming inside and removing the pan from the stove top and setting it aside so the bacon would stop burning.

"So, you and Cal get that pump fixed? I'm assuming since Clint set out about an hour ago that you did, considering he's still alive."

"It was a pain."

"How's the hand after all that?"

"Sore, but nothing too bad."

"What brings you by this morning?" She rested her hands on her hips.

"I came to make sure you weren't burning down my house."

"Oh, right." She grinned sheepishly.

Julia returned wearing a pair of jeans and t-shirt, her hair tied into a messy bun on top of her head.

"You planning on church?" Alice asked him.

"I told Annie I'd be there."

"Good. We'll ride with you. Knock when you're ready for us." She left him standing there and walked to her room to dress and get ready for the day.

Julia looked him over. Weariness still clung to his face, but his eyes were sharp as they looked at her. "Thank you for the meal. You didn't have to do that."

She shrugged. "Figured you might be hungry after a long day and the last thing you'd want to do is cook something."

"You were right. I'm sorry I missed out on a fun night."

"It wasn't much different than the one the other day. But hey, we at least both got out of dancing and bowling."

He smirked. "True."

"Well, I better go clean myself up for church." She motioned over her shoulder. "And then soak that pan." She grimaced.

"Right. Me too. Church, that is." Graham ducked out the door. "If Alice wants breakfast, tell her we'll just leave early and grab a donut or something. I'd rather she not touch the stove."

Julia chuckled. "Will do." Shutting the door and resting her back against it, she sighed. Yes, after an evening surrounded by Hastings brothers, it was nice to see the one that occupied most of her thoughts. She jostled as the door behind her opened. Turning, she was surprised to see Graham had returned and blushing, hoped he hadn't been reading her thoughts.

"This evening I'd like to take you for another ride. If you'll join me."

Her heart skipped as she noticed him wringing his hat in his hands. Was this Graham's version of a date request? She hoped so. "I'd love to."

Slowly, a small smile washed over his face and she realized he'd been nervous she'd say no. Her heart warmed. Nodding, he backed off the porch and walked back towards his house. She realized then that his feet were bare and that he must have sprinted over when hearing the alarm. He'd grabbed his hat, which she thought was humorous, but he hadn't thought about fighting a fire with shoes on. And that made her heart melt a bit more.

∞

The church was a simple, white, wood-framed building with a steeple that reached up into the morning sky. It'd seen better days, weathered by the dust storms she knew blew through west Texas ever so often, but the overall building was charming and inviting. The people welcomed her with smiles and hugs, and as everyone loitered outside of the building, she,

Alice, and Graham waited for the rest of the brothers. They arrived in various vehicles, all except Clint, who was sure to still be working. All of the Hastings brothers cleaned up nicely.

Philip emerged from a group of people a few feet away. "Nice to see you two have survived life on the ranch." He hugged Alice and Julia in welcome.

"That we have."

"No varmints?" he asked Julia.

"Not a one." She smiled up at him.

"Good to hear. Or maybe I spoke too soon?" He nodded in the direction of his brothers walking up. Julia noticed every woman under the age of fifty watch the Hastings show. They didn't do anything to warrant such attention. They simply walked towards the church. But, if she admitted it, that was all they had to do. They looked handsome in their pressed jeans and starched shirts. All had shaved or trimmed their mangy beards over the last few days and looked somewhat recognizable. They wore clean cowboy hats and polished boots, and each had their charming smiles on their faces as they walked up to greet her and Alice.

"That's a pretty dress." Lawrence tipped his hat towards Julia and she smiled in thanks. "You clean up pretty well."

He flushed and Alice laughed. "Maybe I need to invite more pretty friends around so you guys will continue to put forth some effort."

"Give it up, Al," Cal's voice cut through as he walked up. "You know we always look this good."

Alice rolled her eyes. "You may look good, but I've yet to have one of you offer to escort me inside the building this morning."

"As they should." Annie's voice carried over as she extended her arms to her boys. "My, my, my, look at those faces." She grabbed Hayes' chin and surveyed his shaving job. "Smooth as a baby's bottom and as handsome as John Wayne." She kissed him on the cheek and did the same to the other brothers. She reached her hands out to Julia and squeezed them. "You look beautiful, sweetie. I love that dress. White with turquoise is one of my favorite color combinations. You just look so pretty, doesn't she, Graham? Like a postcard." Annie winked at her as she turned around and yelled. "Henry! Come meet Julia!" She stepped to Julia's side as a stocky man of short height, thick glasses, and jolly disposition stomped forward, shaking Hastings hands as he went. He removed his cowboy hat, and the gush of aftershave that seemed to envelope him tickled Julia's nose. He extended his hand. "Nice to meet you, Julia. Annie's told me a lot about you."

"Nice to meet you too."

"You know, I just love Santa Fe." He extended his arm to her, and though she knew that suffocating smell would no doubt cling to her, she couldn't turn down the kind man's offer. Draping her arm through his, she allowed him to escort her inside the church while he spoke of vacationing in Santa Fe thirty years prior. She glanced over her shoulder and her eyes met Graham's.

"I think that is your summons," Annie whispered to him with a small elbow nudge to his side. "Go save her from Henry. And sit by her."

He walked towards the church and Annie slid into step beside Alice. "He always was the first to obey."

Giggling amongst themselves as they entered, Julia and Henry waited to the side of the door. Graham took off his hat and placed it along a wooden shelf that lined the entry hall. Cowboy hats of all shapes, sizes, and colors rested there. Removing their hat inside the building was a small token of respect, but overly charming to see that every man did indeed remove his hat upon entering the building.

"I've never seen that before," Julia muttered to Alice.

"Yeah, I'm surprised it can actually hold the weight of all those big heads."

"Not what I meant," Julia whispered. She silenced when Graham walked up and tilted a nod towards the sanctuary. Her feet, unbeknownst to her brain, immediately stepped to his side and followed him.

H

Chapter Eleven

At the sound of the church bells, the after-church socializing congregants began to drift to their respected vehicles and head for home. Annie hustled after the Hastings brothers and made sure they remembered she'd put a pot roast on for everyone.

"I think I'm going to ride with Annie and Henry," Alice said.

Graham motioned for her to hurry to catch up with them. "We'll be along as soon as I can pry Betty Langley away from Julia."

"Good luck." Alice hurried away.

Graham eased next to Julia and placed a hand at her elbow, Betty's eyes flashing towards the physical contact with interest. A bloom in her cheeks and eyes told him she read more into his move than he intended. "Well, I won't keep you. I see you have more important company to be keeping. You just don't be afraid to show up on Thursday, alright?"

"Yes ma'am." Julia waved in farewell and then looked up at Graham.

"Quilting?" he asked.

"Knitting, actually."

"Do you knit?"

"Absolutely not. But apparently I need to learn, according to Betty."

"In a day. While you're on vacation."

She giggled. "It would seem so."

"We'll just have to make sure you're busy on Thursday evening." He hadn't meant for his comment to sound like he intended to make plans with her, but when he heard it, he felt that gut punch of recognition. He cleared his throat. "Ready to head to Annie's?"

"Yes. When you are. Where's Alice?"

"She already left."

"Ah. Alright."

Graham placed his hat on his head as Julia draped her hand through his arm. "The service was nice," she commented.

"Yeah. It was."

"The whole 'love one another' message speak to you today?" she asked with a smirk. "Meaning Clint."

He gave a fake shudder and she laughed.

"He's alive and well and able to breathe another day. I think he and I are both counting our blessings this morning. He's alive, and I am not a murderer."

Julia grinned. "You've already forgiven him."

"You think so?"

"Yes. You're too much of a family man not to."

"And what gives you that idea?"

"Mr. Head of the Table." She accepted his offer of opening her truck door and hopped inside, buckling her seat belt. When he climbed in, she continued. "The way you try to keep them all in line as best as you can. The way you try to give them work that compliments their strengths. Strengths you see in them. You love them. Deeply. It's obvious, despite your giving them a hard time."

"I guess you're right. Hopefully they see it that way as well."

"They'd be dumb not to."

He liked her perception of him. And though it was true, he wasn't sure his brothers actually did see his actions in the same light as Julia. He turned onto a street and parked along the curb in front of a modest brick home that boasted perfectly groomed flower beds. Despite the summer heat, flowers spilled forth in vibrant colors and the yard, despite a few dry patches, held a luscious green hue.

"Cute house." Julia unbuckled and Graham helped her step down from the truck. Her perfume wafted towards him. She didn't release his hand as they headed towards the house. Instead, she swung their joined hands between them as she pointed out various flowers and named them perfectly. "I like that she planted mostly wildflower combinations."

Graham only half listened. He was too distracted by her hand in his. Thankfully, she'd grabbed his good hand. Annie swung the door open with a wide smile. "You two are the last of them. Come on in. Graham, the men are out back. Julia, I've got an apron in the kitchen for ya. I just have to whip up some mashed potatoes. I've got Alice filling the tea glasses. I'd like for you to cart the desserts to the buffet table outside under the porch."

"Yes ma'am."

"You can boss people around with such finesse, Annie," Graham complimented.

The older woman never broke stride as she nudged him towards the back door and away from Julia. He squeezed Julia's hand one more time, her dark eyes meeting his with a smile that held a shyness he hadn't seen before. Reluctantly, he released her as Annie nudged him out. The older woman wiped her hands together as if she'd dusted off the dirt and planted them on her hips. "Now, let's see, oh yes, potatoes." She pointed towards the desserts: a chocolate cake, two pies, and a pudding and motioned for Julia to start her way outside with them.

Julia hefted the glass bowl with the pudding.

"There's a metal bowl with ice waiting for that, Julia. To keep it cool."

"Yes ma'am." Julia slipped out the back door.

"Did you see that?" Annie asked Alice.

"I sure did."

"Have you talked to her about it?"

"Yep. She denies anything other than being attracted to him."

"Oh posh. There's more to it than that. Graham was holding on to her."

"Yep."

"You talk to him about it?"

Alice grinned. "Yep."

"And?" Annie held the mixer over her potatoes and waited to start mixing so she could hear Alice's response. Julia walked in and Annie waved Alice's attention away and began mixing as if they weren't just discussing Julia and Graham. When Julia exited again, she killed the mixer. "What'd he say?"

"Nothing really. It's Graham. I can tell he likes her, though. We all can. It's just a matter of time."

"But she's only here another week." Annie looked worried as she gazed out the window above her kitchen sink and watched Julia prep the dessert table. "We can't let her slip through our fingers."

"Don't you mean *his* fingers?" Alice asked.

"Right, right, right." Annie waved away her comment.

"Besides, I'm working on that."

"Well, work faster, girl. I've never seen my Graham like this before. Oh, if his momma could see him now. How proud she'd be of the man he is." Sentimentality had Annie sniffing back a tear before continuing to mix her potatoes. She added a pat of butter and continued to mix.

Julia walked back in and waited for the sound of the mixer to cease. When it did, she looked to Annie. "Anything else?"

"Nope. Alice, how are the glasses comin'?"

"All full."

"Perfect, let's go ahead and take them outside and put them at a place setting. We're at the picnic table today."

"Yes ma'am."

Both women scurried to do her bidding.

Annie watched as Graham followed Julia with his eyes and that ever so often Julia raised her own to meet his. Smiling, she picked up the bowl of potatoes and headed outside.

∞

"Oh, come on now there, Lawrence," Henry cut in. "You come here, you eat." He plopped another giant spoonful of potatoes on Lawrence's plate and passed the bowl to Seth. "Besides, nobody makes mashed potatoes like my Annie." He winked at his wife and she flushed at his praise.

"Alright you two, save it for the honeymoon," Philip quipped, accepting the basket of homemade bread from Cal and passing it on to Graham.

Graham placed two slices on his plate and waited patiently as Julia finished her conversation with Alice.

"Oh." She smiled and took the basket. "Thanks." She placed a piece on the side of her plate and spanked Alice's hand when her friend went for three pieces.

"It's Annie's bread," Alice defended her choice. "And you need to eat more than bread, Alice Wilkenson, or you're going to keel over."

Annie chuckled and nodded. "She's right, Alice. Besides, you don't want hips like your momma."

The Hastings brothers all chuckled and accepted the icy stare Alice shot each of them. But she listened and only took two pieces instead of three before passing the basket on.

"And what plans do you girls have for this upcoming week?" Annie asked.

"Not much, really," Alice said. "I've got to work, so on days Julia doesn't want to be in Sheffield, she can float wherever she likes."

"We should dart over to Fort Stockton, Julia. They have some wonderful shops there," Annie mentioned.

"That sounds like fun."

"Unless the boys have something planned for you?" Annie looked to each of the Hastings brothers, most avoiding eye contact. Graham shot her a warning glance and Annie grinned. "We'll pick a day."

"Sounds good to me," Julia agreed, unaware of the Annie/Graham exchange.

"I hate that Clint couldn't make it today," Annie continued. "But that boy needs to learn to handle his responsibilities. Y'all will take him a plate home."

"You spoil us, Annie." Hayes accepted the hand squeeze Annie gave him.

"I love to, you know that. And I'm just happy to see you off that ranch, cleaned up, and interacting with the human race again. Y'all were gettin' too comfortable out there on that ranch by yourselves. I think Alice and Julia's presence out there has shaken things up a bit. Which reminds me, Alice, that house of yours here in town needs to go." Alice opened her mouth to retort, but Annie held up her hand. "Henry took a look at it, and honey, it needs a lot of work. Now, the way I see it is you can either A.) Find you a place in Sheffield, B.) Temporarily live with us, or C.) Live in Graham's guest house. But that little house is not for a young lady anymore." She waved her hand in finality.

"I've been telling her that myself, Annie," Cal added.

"Well, telling her and doing something about it, Calvin Thomas Hastings, are two different things." She pointed her hard gaze from Cal back to Alice. "You understand me?"

"Yes. I'm actually trying to figure that out. Not sure what the plan is going to be when Dad quits the clinic. Best bet would be Sheffield. I just hate leaving Parks."

"Need to find you another vet who will fill your daddy's spot and then you can dart all over the place like you want," Henry chimed in.

"That's a hard search."

"How do you know?" Henry asked. "Have you tried?"

Embarrassment washed over Alice's face. "No."

"There ya go, then. Philip could post something at the feed store, couldn't you, Philip? Folks come from all over to that place."

"I sure can," Philip agreed. "Just let me know what you're after, Al."

She nodded and forked another mouthful of roast.

Annie glanced at the empty plates surrounding the table. "Julia, you mind helping me clear the table?"

"Not at all." Julia swiped her napkin over her lips and slipped out of her seat. She grabbed Graham's plate and placed it on her own before reaching for several more. He stood as she turned with a stack in her arms and grabbed hold of Annie's china before it slipped to the ground.

"I'll take these." Graham slipped them from her grasp and walked towards the house. The other boys began to rise and offer their assistance as well, so as not to be outdone by their older brother.

Annie sat back in her seat and waved Julia down. "And that's how you clear the table," she whispered and winked to the two women.

Julia shook her head on a laugh as the boys walked back, carrying the dessert plates and all the desserts to the picnic table.

"Why thank you, boys," Annie praised as if she were completely unaware of her manipulative tactics. "Y'all are such gentlemen. Come on, girls, we get first dibs." She scooped a hearty helping of banana pudding onto her plate and accepted a small piece of chocolate cake from Henry before delightfully sitting back like a pleased mother hen.

∞

"I am so stuffed." Julia held her stomach as she climbed out of Graham's truck and walked towards the porch of the guest house. Alice had ridden back with Cal and was already standing outside, draping her freshly washed sheets on the line.

"Annie has a way of feeding us for a week in one sitting." Graham stood at the base of the stairs as Julia walked up. He felt himself slipping, not physically, but softening in the presence of others as he watched the swish of Julia's dress as she walked.

She turned and smiled, her hands resting along the porch railing. "What do you have planned for the rest of the afternoon?"

"Nothing really, until later." He slipped his hands into his pockets and rocked back and forth on his heels.

"You actually have nothing to do?" Julia's brows rose. "Zero projects?"

"There's always projects," he said. "But Sundays are for rest. Why?"

She shrugged. "I was just curious."

Alice tried hard not to laugh. She lifted the laundry basket and handed it to Julia on her way into the house. "Your turn. And for goodness sake,

Graham, get a clue." She walked inside and helped herself to the pitcher of tea.

Confused, Graham looked to Julia as she eyed the laundry basket in her arms. "My sheets are in the wash." She set the basket down on the rocking chair. "I've still got a while yet before they're done."

Alice walked behind Julia in the house and moved her fingers like two people walking behind her friend's back. Graham's brow cocked before he focused back on Julia.

"I was just going to change out of these church clothes," he said. "Maybe go for a walk. Want to join me?"

Julia's emphatic head bob and smile eased the tension in his shoulders as he nodded. "I'll be back in a few minutes." He'd barely made it to the porch when he heard Julia's sing-song voice as she bragged to Alice that Graham had asked her for a walk. He bit back a smile. Perhaps she was interested in him after all.

She was sitting on the porch in shorts and a tank top, her hair in a ponytail, a glass of tea in her hand when he emerged from the house. Alice sat in the other rocking chair, an amused smirk on her face when he walked up. "Have her home before dinner, Graham," Alice warned.

"Only so I'll cook," Julia chuckled as she set her cup aside and hopped down the steps towards him. "Where to?"

He motioned to behind his house and she followed along side him. He didn't quite have a plan, but he decided taking her down by the creek might be the best option. It was close, shaded, and offered some good spots to sit should she want to. He'd never walked the ranch with a woman, so he had zero clue as to what she'd find interesting. The pasture behind his house was full of wildflowers, so that at least lent some beauty to the area. She picked a few as they walked.

"In Santa Fe, I like to walk the downtown area on Sundays." She bent to pluck another flower. "Tourists are out and about, but in general the streets aren't as crowded as they typically are throughout the week and on Saturdays. There's a peacefulness to the city on Sundays that I like."

"Do you live in the city?"

"Close, but not downtown. It's too expensive. Apartments are ridiculous in Santa Fe."

"I imagine so. I couldn't imagine living in an apartment building. I'd go crazy."

"It has its moments," she agreed. "When I need space, I just go visit my parents. They live just outside the city."

"Nice having your parents close." A touch of longing was in his voice.

"It is." She smiled up at him. "Most of the time."

"You close with your parents?" he asked.

Pondering his question a moment, she nodded. "I'd say so. I meet with them at least once a week for lunch or dinner. I talk to them every other day or so."

"Any siblings?"

She nodded her head. "Well, I did. Now it is just me. My brother passed away about five years ago."

"I'm sorry to hear that."

"It was hard, for sure, but he died doing what he loved: serving his country. He was in the military. Army."

"Well, I can certainly respect him for that."

"My parents had a hard time for a while. It's one of the reasons I stayed in Santa Fe at the time. But that was five years ago, and I just sort of didn't leave."

"Do you wish you had?"

"Sometimes." Her eyes lit up as she spotted the creek. "Oh, look at that." She hustled towards it. "This is a nice surprise." She sat on the grass and patted the earth next to her. She began sorting through the flowers she had picked. He handed her a handkerchief and she grinned. "Thanks." She dipped the stems into the water and wrapped them tightly into a small bouquet with the handkerchief to keep moisture on them. "You guys have a beautiful place. I can't thank you enough for letting me stay here. It's like an entirely new world for me. I see paintings and photos of cowboys and Native Americans all the time. Horses and longhorns, etc. But to see the real workings of a ranch has been interesting. Not something I could ever experience in Santa Fe. I also can't imagine being in Alice's house with all its issues."

"It's no problem. The guest house sits empty most of the time anyway. I'm glad it's been useful."

"What did you think about Annie offering it to Alice at lunch?"

He eased to the ground beside her, stretched his legs out as she ran her fingers through the creek. "It would help her out."

"True. But you also like your space."

"There is that." He picked a blade of grass and rubbed it between his thumb and pointer finger. "Can you keep a secret?"

Julia leaned back on her haunches and stared at him. "Of course."

"I admit it's been kind of nice having company close by."

"Oh really?" A slow smile crawled over her face as she nudged his shoulder. His lips curved into a smile of their own.

"*Don't* tell Alice. It will go to her head."

She locked her lips with an imaginary key and tossed it into the creek.

"You'll have more fire alarms going off if she stays."

"There is that."

Julia giggled. "Gotta love her."

"We all have quirks, though. Alice is helpful around the ranch. She's pretty much like a sister, so she'll fit in just fine."

"And what quirks do you have?" Julia asked.

"I figured you'd have a long list made out by now."

"And why would I have that? You've been nothing but nice to me."

"I'm glad you think so."

"And you don't? Have you not been?" She chuckled as he met her gaze.

"I don't typically..." He rubbed his chin, his five-o-clock shadow tugging against his palm. "Well, let's just say I struggle with interacting with people. Not quite sure how I come across sometimes."

Her brown eyes studied him closely as he spoke, and he felt an uncomfortable silence stretch between them until she smiled. "You're not as bad as you think you are, and you're not near as bad as people tease you about being."

"That's good to hear." He flashed a relieved smile and tossed the blade of grass to the ground. The sun had started to set, and the pasture skies lit up with radiant colors splashing and slashing through the clouds.

∞

"This is one of my favorite times of day." Julia leaned back on her hands and they both sat staring at the sunset. The sound of the creek splashed near their feet and Julia could just make out the scent of Graham's cologne he'd applied for church that morning. She couldn't think of a more peaceful spot.

"I try to catch sunrise and sunset each day, though I admit sometimes it's just a passing glance."

"The downside of working inside a building all day is that it limits my exposure to pretty clouds and sunshine most days." Julia shrugged. "But I plan to soak in each and every one while I'm in Texas."

"That's why you're on the front porch each morning."

"Yep." She smiled. "The mornings start out soft and then erupt into bright and marvelous colors. The evenings are deeper, richer and just set the mood for cozying up with a blanket. Even when it's a bit warm outside."

"Sunsets are my internal timer to remind me to go home and eat something."

Julia snorted and then laughed as she looked at him.

He grinned and she loved seeing his dimples appear for a moment.

"You have a great smile, Graham."

She sensed her compliment took him by surprise. He grew quiet, a bit antsy, and avoided direct eye contact. Her heart tripped a little further towards the man. As hard and tough as he was, a shyness lingered about him. Leaning towards him she placed a soft kiss on his cheek. "Thanks for the walk." She pushed herself to her feet and reached for her flowers. Graham held them up to her before climbing to his own feet. When he stood, he towered over her, which she liked. He stared at her a moment and then nodded towards the houses. They'd taken a couple of steps when he stopped and gently grabbed her arm, spinning her towards him. Before she could catch her bearings, his lips grazed hers and his hands were gently cupping her face. Regaining her balance, she leaned into him, her own arm linking up and around his neck as he pulled her close and the kiss grew deeper. She tenderly pressed a hand to his chest and nudged him back a moment, reluctantly breaking contact from that serious scowl of a mouth that held such gentleness when it needed to. She rested her forehead against his chest and felt his fingers brush through her ponytail before she peered up at him. Those navy eyes that typically held a quiet fury or restrained temper were soft, vulnerable, and achingly beautiful. She kissed him once more and pulled away from his touch before she completely lost her senses.

Graham reached for her hand, brushing his thumb over her knuckles as he began walking back towards the guest house. Alice was inside at the stove, probably about to burn the house down again. "Want to come inside?" Julia asked.

Graham took a steadying breath. "I better not."

She stood on the top step, he on ground level, which made her eyes level with his. She cupped a hand to his cheek and then lightly brushed her fingertips over his lips. Biting back a smile, she gave into the urge and pressed her lips to his again. One last kiss wouldn't hurt. She felt his hand slip around her waist and pull her close as he slowly walked up the porch steps.

"Hey, do you use sesame oil or fish oil when you're sautéing—" Alice's voice trailed off as she spotted them. "Oh." She darted back into the house, the two on the porch still oblivious to her interruption.

The sound of tires coming up the drive had Graham tugging back and glancing up to see two of his brothers pulling up to the house. "I should go now."

"Yes. You should," Julia agreed, her cheeks a rosy shade of pink for being caught kissing Graham.

"I'll..." Graham stepped down and just stared at her. "I don't really know what to say to you right now, if I'm being honest. Just that... well..." He cleared his throat as his brothers shut their truck doors and walked towards the main house.

"We're here for the weekly update and a beer, Graham," Lawrence called. "Meet ya inside."

Julia watched as his front door closed and then looked down at him again. "You don't have to say anything."

"Yes. I do." Graham rubbed a hand over his jaw and let loose one of his devastating smiles that turned her knees to jelly. "Maybe once my head clears, I can tell you how nice this evening was and that I enjoyed spending it with you."

"I think you just did." Julia gave him an encouraging nod towards his house. "But you can tell me again in the morning." She pointed to her porch. "I'll be right here."

"I like that plan. I'll see you then."

She felt the tingles from her hair down to her toes as he sized her up with one long last glance before turning and heading towards his house. When she stepped inside, Alice waited patiently by the stove, arms crossed over her chest as she leaned against the counter.

"Well? How's Graham?"

Breathless, Julia walked over to Alice and hugged her tight until Alice squirmed on a laugh. "Okay, okay. Get off of me." She swatted Julia. "You're glowing, so I'm assuming you finally planted one on him and it went in your favor."

"Actually," Julia beamed and danced a small jig. "he planted one on *me*." She covered her mouth on a loud giggle.

Alice shook her head and smiled. "I see."

"Oh Alice, he's wonderful." Julia walked towards the counter and grabbed a wine glass and poured. She glanced over at Alice's and topped it off. "We talked, and he actually contributed to the conversation."

"That is big." Alice, impressed, listened as Julia gushed on and on. Her plan of keeping Julia in Texas to help run the clinic was underway better than expected. No, she hadn't planned for Julia to fall for a Hastings brother, she was more hoping to convince her friend to fall in love with the animals at the clinic. But what a bonus if Graham came into the equation. And it looked as if Graham Hastings, whether he knew it or not, was well on his way to making Julia McComas fall in love with him.

H

Chapter Twelve

"*I don't know what* is going on with him today." Seth beat his hat against his leg and plopped it back onto his head, dust settling around his shoulders.

"What do you mean?" Clint looked towards Graham as he talked with Hayes and accepted the reins to an old mare fully dressed in an extra saddle.

"I mean, it's Monday and he's off to go joyriding with Julia."

"That so?" Clint, intrigued, leaned against the fence, his clasped hands hanging over the edge, his boot resting on the bottom rung as they watched their brother lead the horses further out into the pen.

"Yeah. When has he ever done something like this?"

"It would be a first." Clint looked up as Lawrence walked up wiping his hands on his jeans.

"You believe this?" Clint pointed towards Graham as the oldest brother hoisted himself into his saddle.

Lawrence smiled. "Maybe he's wanting to show Julia more of the ranch since Alice wants her to stay in Parks."

"But Graham? Why would Alice choose Graham for a task like that? At least choose the most likeable brother." Seth pointed to himself.

"Or most handsome." Clint pointed to himself.

"Maybe she was going with mature," Lawrence jested as he slipped his gloves on his hands and ducked through the fence to head to the stalls and help Hayes. He stopped to grab a dropped rein and hand it to Graham. "Got you a riding buddy this morning?"

"Julia."

Lawrence, having witnessed Graham and Julia smooching on the porch the evening before, gave his brother a chummy grin. "That so? Plan on sneaking her out to the creek again? Steal some kisses?"

Graham's expression never wavered as he stared at his brother. "Saw that, did you?"

"Just the kiss on the porch, but figured there had to be more than that one based on the way she looked at you."

Graham grunted.

Lawrence held up his hands. "I haven't said anything to the others. Though they're wondering what's got you neglecting work and riding around for fun this morning."

"Horses need some exercise."

"Riiiiight." Lawrence laughed. "Work on that excuse a bit, G."

"It's none of their business. How's that?"

"Rings with more of a Graham attitude. I like it." Lawrence grinned. "And for what it's worth, Graham, I like her too. Now, get. Have fun before I start sulking that I have to muck stalls while you spend time with a beautiful woman."

"I think we're all jealous of that." Hayes emerged and clapped Graham's horse on the rear to send him on his way. "He and Cal deserve a late start today considering they cleaned up Clint's mess with the water pump. So, you really saw them kissing?"

Lawrence nodded. "Oh yeah. It wasn't a little thing either. I think our big brother's officially tangled up in love now."

Hayes laughed. "Power to Julia."

"I know, man. She's tougher than I thought if she can turn Graham to romantic mush."

"Let's not get ahead of ourselves. It was just a kiss," Hayes said. "It will take more than that to convince Graham to take any future steps. He's married to this ranch. And Julia... not sure she's the type of woman who'd be happy out here."

Lawrence lifted his shoulders and let them drop. "We'll see. All I know is that both of them had stars in their eyes yesterday. And if we hadn't driven up to the house, I imagine Alice would have had to hose 'em off."

Hayes smirked. "Now that I would have liked to have seen." He clapped Lawrence on the back as he led him into the horse barn and to their newest addition.

∞

Julia watched as Graham rode up on his horse with another fully saddled next to his. He tied the reins of both to the porch railing before walking up the steps to knock on the door. Her heart hammered in her chest. Just seeing him ride up the lane had her pulse skyrocketing, cheeks flushing, and hands jittering. Did she really kiss him yesterday? Yes. Oh yes, she did. She nibbled her bottom lip at the memory and felt heat rise up her neck. He looked more relaxed this morning, his shoulders not as stiff, his mouth still set in a firm line, but his jaw wasn't clenched. He was at ease coming to her door after their last encounter. He didn't seem nervous to see her, though she felt she would bolt out of her skin the moment he looked at her. What was she to do about these feelings towards him? She was leaving in six days. It wasn't near enough time to truly get to know him, but her heart squeezed at the thought of not seeing him every day. She'd gotten used to seeing the tall and handsome cowboy next door. What would it be like to just see them in photos at the museum? Nothing would ever compare to the sight of the Hastings brothers working out in the fields. No photograph, no painting, no sculpture could capture the strength, determination, and appeal of the real-life version of a working cattleman. She opened the door, his head was down, his hat shading his face. But when he heard the door, he looked up and flashed that quick, knee-weakening smile of his. She was thankful Alice had already left for work that morning so as not to ruin the sweet moment of them just staring at one another. He extended his hand to her and a thrill shot up her arm when she placed hers in his. Another horse emerged on the horizon at break-neck speed and had them watching as Hayes struggled to bring it to a halt.

"Everything okay?" Julia, hand on her heart, started towards the brother but Graham held her back as the horse stomped his feet and turned in fast circles, Hayes's grip on the reins tightening as he continued to command the horse. Finally, the horse stutter-stepped and came to a stop.

Hayes flashed a relieved grin at Graham. "Sorry for the interruption, guys." He patted the horse's neck and heaved exhausted breaths. "This guy is slowly coming to terms with a rider on his back."

"Battle of the wills." Graham nodded in approval. "Good job getting him out of the pen to let him run. Seems it's what he needed."

"Yep. Realized it the other day. He needed to run off some of this pent-up anger."

"We all need to every now and then."

Hayes tipped his hat to Julia. "Mornin', Julia."

She smiled. "I thought there was an emergency. I'm glad it was nothing serious. But you be careful up there, Hayes. That horse doesn't seem too keen on having you in the saddle."

"He'll get used to me."

"Hayes, the horse whisperer," Graham assured Julia.

"I try." Hayes nodded towards the horse designated for Julia. "Trained that one myself.

She's one of the most docile we own. She'll be good for a beginner."

"Thanks." Julia walked towards the horse and brushed a hand down the soft nose. The tan hide was smooth as silk and the horse nuzzled Julia's hand. "She seems to like me."

"She will." Hayes's horse stepped nervously in place. "I think he's got the itch to get moving again. Maybe I'll see you two out there. I'll try to avoid running into you with this guy. Don't want to him to stir the others up. Later." He turned the horse in the direction he'd come and released some pressure on the reins. It was only a matter of seconds before the horse was off in a sprinting gallop. Hayes' hat blew off his head and landed in the driveway, the brother unbothered as he held on tight and let the horse fly.

"He's extremely brave, isn't he?" Julia shook her head in wonder. "I couldn't do that. I'd be scared to death."

"Years of practice. Hayes is the best, though. People travel from all over to let him break and train their horses."

"And whose horse is that?"

"Soon to be mine."

Her eyes widened. "Graham, no." She shook her head and he laughed.

"Why not?"

"That horse is dangerous. And what's wrong with the one you have?"

He lovingly patted his horse. "Trisket's getting a bit old. I want her to have some rest."

"But that death trap?" Julia pointed to the dust cloud that remained from Hayes's journey.

"He's still got some work ahead of him on that one," Graham admitted. "By the time I sit in the saddle, the horse will be docile and manageable. Though, I'm hoping it will keep a bit of the spirit he has. Now come on, let's get you saddled up." He walked her to the side of the horse. "Grip the saddle horn and place your left boot... shoe," he corrected, noticing her foot attire, "into the stir up. Now hoist yourself up." He helped her into the saddle and she nervously gripped the saddle horn with both hands.

"I-I-I don't know about this, Graham."

"You're doing great. Just stay calm and steady." He untied both sets of reins from the porch and hoisted himself into his own saddle. He started to hand her the reins and she shook her head.

"Just give me a second." Julia breathed slow, deep breaths. "It's so high. What if I fall?"

"You won't," he assured her.

"But what if I do? What if she doesn't like me and bucks me off? Or runs like Hayes' horse? I won't be able to hold on like he did." Panic began to rise.

"Julia," Graham waited until she met his calm gaze. "you'll be fine. Now take the reins."

She did and he showed her how to hold them in her hands and how to guide and direct the horse. The horse, named Vivica, was as laid back as Hayes had claimed, for which Julia was extremely grateful. She moved in any direction Julia wished to go, but mostly followed alongside Graham's horse as if they were old friends.

"How are you doing?" Graham asked as they cleared the first pasture and headed onto a grass road towards the next.

"Better. She is sweet. I think I'm getting the hang of it." Julia relaxed in the saddle as they reached an open pasture covered in wildflowers. She noticed Graham's keen eyes surveying the field, no doubt looking for predators of some sort. She liked that he was always on guard. A yell called out and had them both turning in their saddles to see Hayes headed straight for them, his wild horse out of control and the brother barely hanging on.

Julia's horse's ears twitched and nervously trotted to the side and Graham's pulled her nose the opposite direction to avoid collision as Hayes continued his blazing journey towards them. Julia's horse continued to stir, and panic began to rise in Julia's chest. She gripped the reins. "Whoa girl. Easy. Easy." She tried to sound at ease, but the horse jerked her head and as soon as Hayes barreled past them, Julia's horse took off. She screamed as she gripped the reins and tried to halt Vivica. She heard Graham behind her, his horse giving him fits as well, but his didn't erupt into a full gallop. She focused on the fast-moving ground beneath her and felt sick to her stomach. Hayes' horse was already bucking up and down in the pasture, poor Hayes holding on for dear life as he tried to maintain some semblance of control. He was losing. And so was Julia. "Graham!" she screamed, as Vivica raced across the pasture. She felt her hands begin to cramp and one of the reins slipped from her grasp. Embracing the fact she was either going to fall off, pass out, or die, Julia closed her eyes.

She heard the pounding of hooves and turned to see Graham riding up fast, his hand outstretched. "Don't move!" he yelled.

Like she could. It was taking all her might to hold onto the saddle horn and the rein in her hand. Graham's horse fell into step with her own and he leaned over to try and catch her loose rein. Julia prayed he'd be able to grab it. But he missed. He slapped the reins of his own horse to urge it onward to make another pass at her reins. He successfully grabbed it and tugged not only on his own horse's reins but hers as well. The two horses began to slow their paces until finally he was able to bring them to a stop. She dropped her chin to her chest and couldn't help the tears that erupted. Her hands, shaking from the crash of adrenaline that coursed through her veins, lifted from the saddle horn as Graham reached for them. She wasn't sure how he managed to pluck her from her horse, but next thing she knew she straddled his saddle facing backwards, her head buried in his chest and his arms wrapped tightly around her.

∞

Graham clicked his tongue and began to slowly lead the horses towards his brother. Hayes lay on the ground, pounding his fist into the grass.

"You alright?" Graham asked him.

Hayes slowly pushed himself to his feet, his clothes covered in tattered grass and flowers, dirt smudged across his chest, and sweat dripping from his face. "Bruised but not broken. I don't think. He planted a hoof in my thigh." Hayes limped towards Julia's vacant horse. "I told you I hate that horse. How's—" He nodded towards Julia and Graham just shook his head. Hayes sighed in frustration that he'd caused such a dangerous fiasco. Graham rubbed a comforting hand over Julia's back and felt the tremors of fear still radiating through her body. Her hands gripped around him with fists twisted into the back of his shirt.

"Geez." Hayes took a deep calming breath, stretching his back as he guided Vivica slowly next to Graham. "I'm sorry to have come up on you guys like that. I didn't know you'd be on the road. I figured the road would be smoother than the pasture. Guess it didn't matter any way."

"It was an accident."

"I'm going to call it a day." Hayes rubbed a palm over his sore thigh. "Think I need to have this checked out, just in case."

"Take someone with you."

Hayes nodded. He cast one more sympathetic glance towards Julia. "Sorry. Again." He clicked his tongue and diverted Vivica in the opposite direction towards the horse stalls. Graham headed straight to the guest house. When they reached the porch, he halted the horse. "We're back." He felt her grip loosen on the back of his shirt and slowly she raised her dust and tear-stained face to his. He felt his heart drop at the sight and hugged her to him. She willingly went into his arms again. "So sorry that happened, Julia. So sorry."

"I think... I think I'm done riding for today," she murmured and sniffled as he lightly kissed her hair.

"Right. I think we all are. Let's get down." Her grip tightened on his shirt when he started to dismount. "It's alright." He eased her hands free, but she adamantly shook her head not wanting to be left on the horse by herself even for a second. Graham looked around for an alternative solution and found it in Seth when his brother rounded the corner.

"How was the ride?" Seth's smile vanished when he spotted Julia. "What happened?" He ran over and Graham removed Julia's arms from around his waist.

"Seth's got ya, Julia. Just ease on down now." His brother intercepted the trembling woman and tucked her into his side as Graham dismounted.

"Come on, Julia. I've got just what you need right over here." Seth escorted her up the porch of the main house and into Graham's kitchen. Graham followed behind them. Seth eased Julia into a chair. He hurried and filled a glass with water and set it on the table. "Need me to get anything?" Seth asked him.

Graham shook his head. "Ride with Hayes to town. He's injured."

Seth's eyes widened as he nodded. "Sure thing." He hurried out the door and towards his truck.

Graham knelt in front of Julia's chair and grabbed her hands. "I'm so sorry." He rested his forehead on her hands and kissed them when he noticed the blisters that would soon coat her palms.

He felt her run a hand over his hair and he looked up. "I'm sorry too." She shook her head at his questioning glance. "I go all crazy crying on you and can't focus. It was just a big blur. I was holding on and couldn't even think." Her hand shook as she ran it through her wind-crazed hair. "I didn't know what to do."

"You did great." Graham pulled her up and into a hug. "You did great, Julia. You held on and that in itself is a big feat when something like that happens."

"Thank you for saving me."

"Anytime." He heard her sniffle as she attempted a small laugh. "I think I'm going to need a few minutes to calm back down. My legs are still wobbly and my heart is out of whack. That was so scary."

"Take your time. I feel about the same. Come on, I'll walk you home." He hugged her to his side as he made his way towards the guest house. "You need to rest or you'll be sore."

"I'm already feeling a bit stiff," she admitted on a shaky breath as they climbed the steps.

"I'd offer you a shot of whiskey to help, but it's a bit early still."

"I'll be fine."

Already her voice grew distant, as did she once they reached the porch. He had every intention of walking her inside, sitting with her on the sofa, holding her. Comforting her. But it seemed Julia didn't want any more to do with him. "I'll see you later, Graham."

"If you need anything—"

"I'll be fine." She forced a watery smile and gently closed the door.

He snatched his hat off his head and tossed it on the ground in a fit. So much for his grand plan of riding around the ranch. Of impressing Julia. Of making her fall in love with the place. With him. He stopped short at that thought, and it only made him angrier. The chances of that happening were now zero. He stared at the closed door before bending down and retrieving his hat and plopping it on his head. He mounted his horse and set out towards the stalls. He'd keep busy, as he always did. Chores and projects. If Julia needed time to relax, he'd give it to her. He needed time too. Space, even. He'd acted like a love-sick fool this morning. He should have considered a shorter ride for her on her first try. Maybe around the pens. Not an open stretch. But he'd been too eager to see her face light up at the sight of the wildflowers or even at him. He couldn't wait to kiss her again and hold her. He was blinded and stupid. Cursing himself for being such an idiot, he kicked his heels and set out in a full gallop.

H

Chapter Thirteen

The next morning Julia busied herself at the vet clinic in Sheffield. She hadn't seen or spoken to Graham since the horse incident. She did know Alice ranted at him for taking her outside the pens on her first ride, but other than that face-off, Julia hadn't heard or seen any sight of him. She regretted avoiding him, but she was embarrassed by her reaction to the situation. She had cried like a sobbing pile of wimp. He probably thought she couldn't hack life on the ranch. If she couldn't even go on a simple horse ride, what use was she? Humiliated at the thought, she huffed and ran a hand over her face before leaving the front desk to grab a soda in the break room.

"That's your second one today." Alice paused in the doorway, her lab coat covered in dark fur. She slipped it off and walked it over to a washing machine and tossed it in. Grabbing a fresh coat off a hook, she slipped it on. "What's eating you today?"

"It's nothing."

"Julia, you never drink soda. The only time I've ever seen you drink them was during finals in college. What gives? Graham?"

Julia avoided eye contact.

"Ah, so it is about Graham. What'd he do now?" Alice eased onto a bench.

"You have patients out there, ya know."

"There's one. And it's Mr. Smithson. I do not deal with Mr. Smithson's dachshunds. So I have all the time in the world." She forced a smile.

"Graham hasn't done anything to me. I haven't even spoken to him since yesterday."

"Then why so glum? And if you say it's because you miss him, I'm going to vomit on this floor and make you clean it up."

A smile tugged at the corners of Julia's lips. "I'm a fool, Alice. That's all. I've recognized it and I'm just trying to come to terms with it. That's all."

"A fool about what?"

"To think a man like Graham could be with a woman like me."

"Why do you say that? Is this about the horse incident yesterday?"

Julia nodded. "I'm just not cut out for ranch life, I guess. He deserves someone who is."

"First off, Graham is a grown man and can decide for himself who and what he wants in a lady. Second, you're being too hard on yourself. It was your first time to ride a horse, and then Hayes had to ruin it. You would have been fine if he hadn't lost control of the beast they call 'potential.'"

"That's just it, though. I completely lost it. I was terrified. And I have zero desire to ride again. I don't want to. At all. And I know that's important to Graham."

"Is it? Have you asked him that?"

"Well, no. But it will be. It's a huge part of who he is. And I imagine he has hopes of one day riding around the ranch with the woman of his dreams. And he deserves that. I'm just not her. It was silly of me to let my emotions get the better of me anyway. I barely know him."

"And yet, here you are talking like you know him well enough to decide his future." Alice rolled her eyes. "I think you're being too hard on yourself. And I think you're not giving Graham nearly enough credit. If you care for him, which I know you do— I can tell— then you need to tell him all this. He'll understand. And who knows, in the future, maybe you will crawl back up in the saddle. It's just not for today. Go home. We're pretty much done here anyway. Go back to the house and talk to him."

Dread pitted in her stomach.

"And don't be embarrassed or weird about it, just tell him your feelings. Graham's a good guy, Julia, he'll listen. And better yet, he'll understand."

"But what if I do tell him I'm scared of horses now and that I don't want to ride and he decides I'm just a waste of time? That I'm too 'city' for him."

Alice laughed. "Then come tell me. I'll tell his brothers. And if one of them doesn't take advantage and propose to you on the spot, I'll beat them all up."

Julia set the half empty can of soda on the counter. "I guess you're right. About talking to him, not the proposal bit."

Alice grinned. "Seth's pretty smitten with you."

Julia ignored her comment as she grabbed her purse. "I'll make dinner tonight. Hopefully at Graham's. I'll try to have it ready by the time you get home."

"I cannot say no to that. Good luck." Alice stood and walked back into the office area, striking conversation with Mr. Smithson and the mini, spoiled dogs she dreaded so much.

∞

He saw the little red Honda as he pulled up the drive and knew Julia must already be home from Sheffield and working with Alice. His stomach tightened as he saw her sitting on the porch, rocking quietly in her chair with Curly contentedly curled in her lap, lavishly accepting every stroke her beautiful hands offered. He shut his door. There was no pretending he didn't see her. He had. And it'd be rude to just walk on by. But he wasn't sure if his presence was welcomed. It was clear she'd been needing her space. She waved and some of the tension in his gut eased.

"How was your day?" she asked.

"Dirty." He glanced down at his shirt. "Cleaning out the tack room with Hayes. You?" He walked up and she lifted a glass of sweet tea towards him that was more than half full. He graciously accepted and took a long pull.

"Good."

Not as much detail as Julia would normally share, but he'd take it and see where it led. "How are you feeling?"

Julia diverted her gaze to Curly and after a couple of smooth pets looked up at him again. "That's a bit of a more complicated topic." A nervous smile ticked across her face.

He eased into the second chair. "Tell me anyway."

She reached for his hand and he gladly accepted, lifting it to his lips and kissing her palm. Her eyes softened, but held a touch of sadness to their dark depths.

"I feel like I've let you down."

"Let *me* down?" Surprised, he angled towards her, resting his elbows on his knees as he listened. "How so?"

Sighing, she nudged Curly to the porch and faced him square on. "Because I'm not sure if I like horseback riding. I mean, I'm officially terrified of the idea. And it's important to you."

He squeezed her hand. "Is that it?"

"Well, yeah, mostly." Julia ran a hand through her hair and gazed out over the scenery, lifting a hand to wave at Lawrence as he passed by in his truck headed towards home.

"You haven't let me down."

Her eyes turned to him again. "I haven't?"

"No." He chuckled and kissed her hand again before releasing it. He stood to his feet. "My momma, rest her soul, married my tough, rough, and sometimes calloused daddy and she never once slipped her foot in a stirrup." He flushed when he realized what he'd said. "I mean, not that we are—" He motioned between them and she waved her hand for him to continue with his story and not backpedal. He cleared his throat. "But they still had fun together, loved each other, had plenty to keep their hands full." He pointed at himself and the next brother's truck that was headed towards home. "You're right, horses are important to me. I love them. I love riding them. I feel like there's no better perspective to see the ranch than on the back of a horse. But, that's *me*. Seth hates riding horses. Cal tries to avoid it any chance he gets, and Philip... I'm not sure how much I'd have to pay him to climb back in the saddle. It's not for everyone, Julia. I'm not disappointed. If anything, I completely understand why you feel the way you do. You had a terrible first experience. If you decide to ride again, it's going to take some time. But if you decide not to, I understand that too."

"Really?" Hope lit her face as she stood and walked towards him, hands wringing in front of her. He tugged her towards him and wrapped his arms around her. When she relaxed in his embrace, he rested his chin on her hair.

"Really."

"Thank you, Graham." She looked up at him and slid one of her arms free so as to place her hand on the side of his face. Her eyes bore into his a moment before she kissed him sweetly on the mouth. She then rested her head against his heart once more and sighed. "It's not such a bad perspective of the ranch from here either," she said as they both looked out over the land and could hear the familiar sound of cows bellowing in the distance.

"Have you made dinner plans?" he asked.

"Other than I know I'm cooking for Alice, no. I can add you to the list, if you like?"

He smiled down at her. "I would. Hastings, party of one, please."

She grinned and slipped from his hands. "Then you go shower. You kind of smell."

He blanched a moment and she giggled. "Don't worry, I like it. But go shower. I'll start supper, and maybe by the time Alice drives up it will be finished."

"Sounds like a plan. You feel better?"

"Much," she assured him and kissed his cheek before he walked towards his house. He turned at his front door and saw Julia waiting at her own and his heart did a funny dance it'd never done before. Uh oh. There could only be one thing that made a man's heart do that, and as he watched her walk inside the guest house, his heart longing for her to be in *his* house, he knew exactly what it was. He'd gone and lost his heart to Julia McComas.

∞

Her days were split between the vet clinic in Sheffield and life on the ranch. She'd successfully learned what 'working the garden with Seth' meant, she'd explored Calvin's 'mechanical palace' as he called it, Lawrence had let her feed a few calves that were orphaned, and she loved that he kept them in his backyard instead of a tiny pen. She learned what mucking stalls truly meant while helping Hayes and even had the courage to brush down a couple of horses, though she still had no desire to ride one. Philip had come by for supper with Graham one night to go over numbers for upcoming orders to save his brother a trip to town. Clint, who'd been scarce around Graham since the well pump incident, buzzed through to flirt and tip his hat a couple of times, even leaving her and Alice a bag of jerky he'd had processed at the meat market in Sheffield. Each brother charmed her with their personality, and she'd grown to enjoy each and every one of them. Alice, sad Julia would be leaving the next morning, had planned a big night out at Sloppy's, but Julia opted out. On her last night in Parks, she wanted to be right here on the 7H, with her boys. Annie and Henry drove up and naturally Annie came bearing gifts of pies, puddings, and cakes to celebrate the occasion, though Julia's heart didn't feel much like celebrating, but mourning. She wasn't ready to head back to Santa Fe. There was more she wanted to do here in Parks and at the ranch.

First, she'd never made that shopping trip into Fort Stockton with Annie, and boy, would she love to pick that woman's brain on life in Parks. Secondly, she'd enjoyed the slower pace of life on the ranch. The beautiful sunrises and sunsets, the companionship of the brothers. Third, Alice still needed help at the clinic, and Julia thoroughly enjoyed her time there. And fourth— She watched as Graham intercepted Annie, relieving her of her pies and accepting the motherly pat to his cheek as the woman hurried into his house. The man across the lawn had bewitched her in the last week. She'd already calculated how often she could drive back to Parks to visit and stay within her budget. She hadn't asked him yet if he'd drive up to Santa Fe to visit her. She wasn't quite sure she'd like the answer, knowing he was tied to the ranch every day. But she couldn't give up on what they had started. She hadn't felt this way about anyone before, and it seemed foolish to walk away as if it were just meant to be a week-long fling. She had to try and make something work. If he wanted to as well, she reminded herself.

Sloppy, better yet, *Ruby*, Julia thought, pulled into the drive and had Lawrence and Seth offering their services to help unload whatever treats she'd brought to the party.

When Alice pulled in from work, her truck clanking up the drive with a new and terrible sound, Calvin waited, impatiently, hands on his hips, no doubt about to lecture her on the maintenance of the vehicle. As soon as Alice's door opened, the bickering started, and Julia grinned at the predictability. Despite his agitation, the brother still offered to unload the cases of beer Alice had picked up on her way home. Cowboys and beer, Julia thought. Their remedy to a long day, a celebration, a tough day, or even just a lazy afternoon. Julia placed the finishing touches onto her outfit, a pair of dangling turquoise earrings and matching bracelet. Alice would tease her later for going to such measures for the Hastings family, but Julia didn't care what any of them thought except Graham. She wanted to look beautiful for Graham. Their last evening together before she left, she wanted to leave a lasting impression for him. Maybe he'd miss her as much as her heart ached at missing him. She'd grown accustomed to his serious face and cherished that gorgeously rare, knee-weakening smile of his, his strong hands that treated her so gently, and his dedication to his family and friends that constantly kept him on his toes. She walked over to the main house and opened the door, stepping into a loud kitchen full of busy bodies and commands, Annie and Alice at the forefront. Hayes spotted her first and crossed his eyes as if the madness of the room had started to take effect. She grinned as Clint walked towards her and offered his arm. "Let me direct you, Ms. Julia, to the living room. There's nothin' but cranky women and dumb men in the kitchen at the moment."

"I heard that," Alice yelled, before she waved him onward.

Ruby sat on the couch and beamed when Julia joined her. "Escape with me," the pixie invited. "If I'm not at the restaurant, I avoid kitchens at all cost."

"Smart."

"Everyone's a little tense in there. Graham, mostly. He wants everything to be perfect." Ruby laughed. "He forgets he's kin to a bunch of Hastings. It's not going to be perfect."

"They're all sweet for wanting to do something special for me."

"That is definitely true. The Hastings boys are definitely sweet. Speaking of..." Ruby pointed to Graham as he shoved Lawrence out of the way so he and Calvin could extend the dining table and add extra leaves for sitting room. "You and Graham going to continue this little spark you have going?"

"I'm not sure. We haven't really had a chance to talk about it."

"Well, you leave in the morning, better get on it."

"I know."

"Just so you know," Ruby patted Julia's knee. "I've known the Hastings brothers my whole life, and Graham has never acted this way. He's never been serious about a woman before. All work for him. But he's a dedicated man. To his family, his community, this ranch. If he decides he wants to make it work with you, Julia, you'll never have to worry about his dedication. Long distance can be tough, but I think it'd be doable with a man like Graham."

"Thanks, Ruby."

The friendly red lips parted into a smile. "And thank *you* for always calling me Ruby instead of Sloppy." She giggled as her nickname was yelled by Seth from the kitchen and he waved her over. Sighing, the woman set her glass of tea on the coffee table. "If only the rest of them would get the memo," she murmured on a laugh as she stood and walked to see why she was needed.

A few minutes later, Graham walked up and helped Julia to her feet. "Your dinner awaits."

"You guys were fast."

"Thank Annie for that." Graham led Julia to the kitchen. No one stood there but her and Graham. Everyone else was seated at the long table, crowded, but happy. Graham pulled the chair out next to his at the head of the table, and they squeezed in next to each other.

"To Julia." Alice raised her glass. "My best friend. My hard worker, for whom I'm still bitter is leaving... and my confidant." She winked at Julia. "We love you."

Everyone toasted their glasses her direction.

"Now let's eat." Alice handed the plate of steaks to Graham, so he and Julia had first pick. An honor, Julia knew, when sitting around a table of hungry men. She'd miss the rowdy bunch, their teasing and elbow jamming already receiving scolds from Annie and Henry as plates were passed and dishes exchanged. She smiled as she looked at each person, her eyes ending on Graham. He'd been watching her study his family and friends, and when she met those dark blue eyes of his she leaned forward and kissed him on the spot, despite the immediate teasing that came from his brothers.

∞

It'd been two weeks since Julia headed home to Santa Fe. Two long weeks of adjusting back to the solitude of quiet mornings. Alice never sat on the porch of the guest house to catch the sunrise and offer him a morning send off. She didn't wait for him to arrive home to make dinner and enjoy a glass of wine on the porch and watch the sunset. Alice was just Alice. Workaholic, high-strung, no-nonsense, Alice. And though she had chosen to take up temporary residence in the guest house, it wasn't the same without Julia. For either of them.

Sure, he and Julia had phone conversations. Long ones at that, which surprised him. He didn't think he'd have much to talk about with someone other than his brothers, but their conversations flowed easily. He liked hearing about her day, about the tourists she encountered, the exhibits she'd been helping set up. But he missed seeing her. He missed how she'd sit and smile as he complained about one of his brothers, knowing full well they had plenty of reason to complain about him. The light scent of her flowery perfume, the way she gently brushed her fingers down his arm right before she'd slide her hand in his. Little things that he hadn't realized felt so nice to have.

"Earth to Graham." A leather rein flung out and caught him on the back of the thigh with a pop. Jumping, he turned to viciously attack the culprit. Hayes grinned wickedly as Calvin rewound the rein and hung it on the wall. "Thinkin' 'bout Julia again?" Calvin asked.

"No."

"Liar." Hayes laughed as he tucked his work gloves into his back pocket.

"I'm not lying."

"Through your teeth," Hayes continued. "You get all soft and doe-eyed when you are."

"You couldn't even see my face," Graham growled, as he stormed towards the square hay barrels and began to disperse some fresh straw in the stall for Trisket.

Lawrence's head popped up over the side of the stall next to his and Graham bit back an oath as his younger brother wriggled his eyebrows. "When you just going to admit it, Graham? You love her. We all see it."

Graham continued dispensing hay. Lawrence flashed an annoyed glance at his other two brothers.

"Alright, fine." Lawrence held up his hands. "I wasn't going to do this, but seein' as how you're not going to act upon anything, I'm callin' her up." He fished in his pocket for his phone. "Going to ask her on a hot date."

"She's in Santa Fe." Graham ignored him.

"So? A woman like that... I'd travel for her." Lawrence pretended to search through his cell phone for Julia's number. "Ah. There it is."

Graham pinned him with an icy stare that quickly dissolved when an actual voice could be heard on the other line.

"Well, hi there, Ms. Julia. Lawrence Hastings here. You know, the cute one." He beamed as Graham made a swipe for the phone and missed. Lawrence ducked away and down into his stall so as to avoid the next attack. "My, it sure is nice to hear your pretty voice."

Hayes and Calvin laughed as Graham grew madder and Lawrence continued his over the top flirtation.

"Oh, I'm doin' just fine. Thanks for askin'." He winked at his brothers. "Say, I've been needin' to make a trip to Santa Fe, been puttin' it off for weeks, you know, due to ranch work. Graham sure keeps me busy." He paused and peeked a glance over the side of the stall, Graham nowhere to be seen. Lawrence's brow furrowed until he felt and smelled the horse dung being dumped on top of him. Howling and trying to swat it out of the back of his shirt and off his neck, he lost his grip on his phone as Graham wrenched it free, Hayes and Calvin bursting into fits of laughter as Graham tried to salvage the conversation.

"Sorry about that, Julia, my brother had a moment of insanity."

Her light giggle lifted his face into a smile. "And why is Lawrence calling me, Graham?"

"To be a nuisance."

"I see." She patiently waited for more of an explanation.

For privacy sake, and so as to avoid more teasing, Graham stepped out of the horse barn. "Seems I'm a bit obvious with my... missing... you." Even the words coming from his own lips felt awkward, but they were the truth.

"Is that so?" Her voice lifted. "I miss you too. Perhaps we should remedy that soon. It's been a couple weeks. I might be able to swing a trip to Parks this coming weekend."

"I hate you driving all the way out here."

"Graham..." She paused a moment, a muffled conversation on the other end telling him she was stepping away from whatever work Lawrence had interrupted. "Sorry about that, it's a busy day."

"You can call me later."

"No, it's okay. It's technically my lunchtime anyway. So, about this weekend? I could leave early on Friday, maybe be there by mid-afternoon."

"Or..." He inhaled a deep breath, rubbing his hand over the back of his neck as he contemplated leaving the ranch for an entire weekend. "I could come see you. There. In Santa Fe."

"You would come here?" The surprise in her voice made the decision easy. He'd drive there every weekend if it meant seeing her face to face.

"Yes."

"Oh, Graham, that would be wonderful!" The smile in her voice relaxed his shoulders.

"Then it's settled. I'll aim for late afternoon then."

"Are you sure you can be away from the ranch?"

"I think out of six brothers at least one of them could manage things while I'm gone."

"Calvin," they both stated at the same time and Julia giggled.

"I can't wait to show you around. I'm sure you've been here before, but I can't wait to show you my favorite spots in the city."

"Sounds like a plan then."

A door opened and a range of voices flooded the line, the clink of dishes and conversation interrupting their phone call. "I need to order a sandwich and get back. Call me Friday when you head out, okay?"

"I will."

"And Graham?"

"Yes?"

"I can't wait to see you." And with that, Julia hung up, leaving him rocking on his heels, a thousand thoughts swarming through his mind. When he turned to head back into the barn, his brothers all stood outside, leaning against the red siding, arms crossed, cheesy grins plastered on their faces, and all eager to hear about his plans.

He pointed a finger at them. "Don't even start."

Laughing, Hayes slapped him on the back as they walked back into the barn.

"Wait 'til Clint hears about this," Lawrence muttered to a serious Calvin. Noticing his brother's stoic face, Lawrence stopped in his tracks. "What's the matter?"

Calvin, speechless over the thought of Graham actually taking a weekend off, much less for a woman, had him shaking his head in disbelief. "I think our brother has officially been shot by Cupid's arrow."

"Great, isn't it?" Lawrence grinned as he darted into the barn to further the teasing of Graham.

Calvin lingered a moment longer, still in shock that Julia had accomplished what no woman had ever done before. Graham was almost human now. The last two weeks he'd been quieter than even his usual temperament. Weighing his options most likely. Figuring the details out. Graham Hastings wouldn't fall in love with someone without weighing and measuring every option and detail. The fact he planned to drive to Santa Fe for an entire weekend said he'd made up his mind that Julia was worth the effort, time, and pursuit. Calvin thought she might be, but he'd never in a million years thought Graham would be the first brother to fall head over heels in love. With a city woman at that. Calvin's lips twitched at the thought of the fun road ahead for Graham and Julia. And, he figured, for the rest of the brothers. They'd have a sister now. A womanly presence in their midst. Well, other than Alice. Just how was this all going to play out?

7H

Chapter Fourteen

Two weeks. Three weeks. A month. Now two months had passed since Julia said her farewells at the 7H Ranch and Parks, Texas. The phone calls from Graham hadn't stopped, but his first trip to Santa Fe never panned out due to Seth's rotating cows to a new pasture and missing a few calves. Naturally, Graham saddled up and helped finish the job, which took him and Seth longer than intended. Since then, she'd been busy; he'd been busy. Their lives operated in two separate circles that never seemed to conjoin to form one of those lovely little Venn Diagrams she'd always been such a fan of. Instead, the phone calls were more frequent but shorter in length. Hurried. As if they were trying to hold onto what little thrill they'd experienced in those two weeks, despite time interfering, and the reason for the thrill had started to fade. However, they'd grown to know one another more intimately. Deeper than she expected over the course of the short phone calls. They *needed* to see one another if this, whatever it was, was meant to happen.

Alice beckoned her to just take the plunge and move on down to Parks, but that was due in part to the fact her dad how now retired, and she felt swamped at the clinic. Though she didn't doubt Alice genuinely wanted her help and company, Julia wasn't quite ready to make that jump if she and Graham couldn't seem to figure out a path forward. Still too many unknowns. And as crazy as she was about him, she still wasn't quite sure he felt the same. His emotions and feelings weren't at the top of his list to openly discuss.

She slid the freshly copied sign-in sheets onto a clipboard and placed it by the front entrance of the museum. People from all over signed their names and where they'd traveled from to the record. She loved perusing that list at the end of each week. She especially loved when she spotted non-residents of the U.S. She loved that her beloved city was a must-see on their list. She picked up the sheets from the previous week and clipped the current day's sign-in sheet to the front of the new stack. Her eyes traveled down the page. California, Oklahoma, Arizona, a handful from various Texas cities, and... she paused, her heart skipping a moment when *Parks, Texas* appeared in scratchy handwriting. She slid her finger to the left to see the name and paused. *Hello, Beautiful* was written in the same script. She looked up, turning in circles to survey the room to see if Graham lurked anywhere. He was nowhere to be seen. She rushed over to the front desk where Tabitha, her boss, stood clicking away on the computer. Beneath black framed glasses, Tabitha's sharp blue eyes darted up towards Julia. She paused. "What's wrong?" Concern had her removing her glasses.

"Have you seen a man come inside? Tall. Cowboy hat, most likely. Ummm…. a scowl on his face."

"I'm not sure…" Tabitha's concern turned to worry. "Are you alright? Is he someone we need to contact security about? I could have them do a sweep."

"No, no!" Julia waved her hands. "That's not necessary. I… he signed in and I don't know where he is."

"Maybe he's actually doing what tourists do here, Julia." She pointed across the room to a group of people studying one of the various paintings displayed.

Julia exhaled, disappointed. He'd come and hadn't found her. Why would he stop by and not say hello? Maybe he was outside. She tapped her hand on the desk. "I'll be right back." She darted out the double doors and glanced up and down under the covered porch. Graham was nowhere. Now she was just getting mad. She crossed her arms and on a defeated sigh walked back into the museum.

Gasping, she froze. Graham stood in the middle of the room, a bouquet of flowers in his hand, and with that sweet, familiar 'I'm-uncomfortable-so-hurry-up-and-take-these-flowers' look on his face. Squealing, Julia ran towards him and jumped into his arms. She pulled back long enough to plant a solid kiss on his lips, as the tourists all turned with interest to the public display. Julia slid to her feet and accepted the flowers with a flush to her cheeks. "What are you doing here?" Searching his face, she loved the small sparkle in his eye as he leaned down towards her and kissed her lightly on the lips.

"I was hoping that was quite obvious." He pointed to the flowers and Julia laughed, hugging him again.

She held a hand to her flamed cheek and motioned for him to follow her towards Tabitha. She made a quick introduction but the two seemed familiar enough already. "Wait," Julia pointed a finger between the two of them. "you knew he was here?"

"Yep. Why do you think I made you print copies of the sign-in sheet?" Tabitha chuckled as she held up an entire fresh stack next to her.

"I wondered how we'd used those up already." Julia shook her head and looked up at Graham in disbelief.

"So, do you typically describe me as wearing a scowl?" Graham asked.

Julia blanched as she didn't know how to respond. It wasn't until she saw his lips twitch that she knew he wasn't offended. "Well, it is a bit of your signature."

"Go." Tabitha waved them towards the door. "I've got the rest of the day. It was nice to meet you, Graham. Finally."

Graham nodded as he tugged on Julia's hand and led her outside and down the steps.

"Why didn't you tell me you were coming? What made you decide to come? When we talked yesterday you had some conference you were headed to." Rattling off question after question helped ease her nerves. Feeling his hand in hers, seeing him again, her heart racing in her chest at the sight of him, had her continually reminding herself he wasn't a dream.

"I had to make you think I was busy." He waited at the base of the stairs as she continued to gawk at him. "Well?"

"Well, what?" Nervously, she hugged him again and rested her head against his chest. "I'm still in shock. Give me a second to just soak you in."

"Now you see why I didn't come right up to you. I needed to just soak you in a bit before I made my move."

She nibbled her bottom lip to bite back what felt like the thousandth smile since she'd laid eyes on him mere minutes ago. She pulled away. "Okay, you're real. I just needed to make sure."

His rare smile flashed as he pointed towards the curb and her parents stood waving.

"What? What are they doing here?" she asked.

"Thanks to Tabitha, I was able to reach out to them a few days ago."

"You... you called my parents?"

He looked down at her. "Is that okay?"

"Yes." Her head bobbed as she welcomed her parents with a hug and watched in wonder as her dad shook Graham's hand as if they were old friends. Her mother, Pam, fluffed the tips of Julia's hair as she leaned in close to whisper. "He's a dream, Julia. An absolute doll." She winked as Julia's dad led the way to her favorite café, Frank's, just up the block near the Daulton Gallery her friend Caroline managed. Matilda waved as they entered, and Julia slid into the seat nearest Graham.

"How long are you here for?" Julia looked at him expectantly as he removed his cowboy hat and placed it on his knee.

"Just until Sunday. I can't be gone too long or Calvin will kill Seth or Clint."

She reached over and squeezed his hand. "I cannot tell you how happy I am to see you." Relief and happiness washed over her as Matilda delivered their drinks and wandered away.

"You don't have to. I feel the same. It's been too long. We need to do better."

"Yes, we do."

"You know," Her dad, Rodney, looked to Graham and gave a small nod before continuing. "you two wouldn't have to go so long between visits if you moved to Parks."

Baffled and slack-jawed, Julia studied her dad as he snuck a wink towards Graham.

"But I couldn't. Not right now, anyway. I mean... my work."

"Sounds like Alice could sure use some help," her mother quipped. "You two are so close, you're like sisters. I know she'd just love having you back."

"But—" Turning, she looked at Graham. He quirked a brow. "And what do you have to say about all this?" She waved her hands towards her parents as she analyzed his face for any type of positive sign or affirmation.

"You have a place to stay," he added.

That was it? That was all he was going to say? Frustrated, she combed her fingers through her hair and leaned back in her chair. She felt him gently grab her left hand and something slid onto her left ring finger. Looking down, her eyes quickly bounced up back to his.

"Could I possibly persuade you, Julia?" Graham rubbed his thumb over her knuckles. "I'd love for you to come to Parks, but only if it's what you truly want. I'm not asking you to marry me. Yet." He clarified and flashed a quick grin at her dad. "I just want to make you a promise that it's on my radar should you want to walk this path with me too. I know I don't have much to offer. I'm grumpy half the time, I have six annoying and *nosy* brothers... but I can promise you that I will care for you and love you, give you a home. It's not the same without you there anyway. Even Alice has turned sour since you left."

Julia smirked at that along with her parents.

"But I want you to know, that no matter what you decide right now, Parks or no Parks, I'm in this with you. I promise." He rubbed his thumb over the turquoise ring that graced her finger. She knew he'd found it locally, based on the craftsmanship and quality. He knew she loved turquoise. It was practically all she wore, and she loved that he embraced that small detail about her.

"You love me?" She quieted a moment and watched as emotions stormed through those navy eyes she loved so much.

"I do. As crazy as it sounds to my own ears, I do. I never thought I would find someone that I'd care for as much as I do you. Even in the small amount of time we shared on the ranch, the ups and downs of you almost making me slice my hand off." She giggled and swatted him on the arm as he grinned. "I think I'd like to have you around a bit more. Longer perhaps. Maybe forever, if that's alright with you? I just figured we'd take it one step at a time. Acclimate you to the place, see if it is somewhere you feel you could be happy. And me... to see if you could be happy with me. Because I don't want you to be there unless you can be truly happy with the ranch, my family, and with me."

Julia's mom dabbed a tear from her eye as both her parents waited on the edge of their seats to hear her response. "I think..." She paused a moment to clear the tears from her throat. "I think I would like to give it a shot too."

Relief flashed across Graham's face as her mother clapped and her dad laughed as Graham's shoulders significantly relaxed. He kissed her solidly on the lips and held her hand over his heart, the erratic beating matching her own. His smile, the radiance of it, she knew she'd never forget. He grabbed his cell phone and dialed a number, placing it on speaker phone as he rested it on the table.

Alice's voice drifted over the line. "Well? How badly did you screw it up?"

Julia laughed. "He didn't. Looks like I'm coming to Parks, Wilkenson."

Hoots and hollers sounded through the speaker, and Julia beamed at the fact all of Graham's brothers had been eagerly awaiting her response as well.

"We love you, Julia," a voice called out.

"That'd be Seth," Alice explained.

"Leave now, Graham, before she changes her mind!"

"And that was Lawrence," Alice continued and then shushed the remaining brothers that tried to get a word in. "Your room is ready and waiting, now get your butt over here, missy. Oh, and you're hired."

Shaking her head, Julia leaned her head on Graham's shoulder and smiled lovingly at her parents. This is what happiness felt like, she thought. The man she loved next to her. Her parents beaming with excitement. And her best friend eagerly awaiting her return.

∞

Three Weeks Later

"If you don't get that horse out of sight right this minute, I'm going to hog tie you in its path of destruction," Graham barked, pointing at Hayes and yet another one of his wild and new additions to the 7H. "I don't want Julia having PTSD the moment she arrives with her parents. Annie!" he yelled.

Annie popped her head out of the main house. "What is it, Graham?"

"The guest room ready for Julia's parents?"

"It sure is. Fresh flowers and all. I also left them a little gift basket on the bed."

"Good. Calvin!"

"Graham." Annie rested a hand on his arm and lovingly tugged at the collar of his shirt as if straightening his buttons. "Leave your brothers alone. Just because you're nervous doesn't mean you have to be a grump to everyone around you."

"I'm not nervous. Why would you think I'm nervous?"

"Honey, you are sweatin' like a summer sun that's just begun to drip dry. Calm down. Alice said they should be here in about ten minutes. Everything is ready. I've got dinner prepped and just waiting on their arrival to throw the steaks on the grill, which Clint will be in charge of."

Graham shot her a panicked look and she tsked her tongue. "He asked for the responsibility and I gave it to him. He's proving himself, Graham."

"Well, if he ruins dinner, I guess we can always go to Sloppy's."

"Ruby's," Annie corrected. "Oh, good. Look, here they come." A dust cloud billowed behind Julia's red Honda as she drove up to the main house and parked next to his work truck. Pam and Rodney emerged from the car as well, as Alice's truck zoomed up behind them in a whirlwind.

Julia ran towards Graham and jumped into his arms, wrapping her own around his neck and planting a kiss on his lips. Though it forced him to show affection in front of his brothers, he didn't mind it. A woman like Julia deserved to be kissed thoroughly and as often as possible. And praise God, he was the man to do it. He shook Rodney's hand and motioned everyone inside.

"We'll fetch the bags," Calvin called to them and he and Lawrence made quick work of removing all the luggage from Julia's trunk. The rest of her belongings would arrive later in the week.

Graham watched as Julia's mother surveyed each of his brothers as they entered and introduced themselves. When Hayes walked inside, dirty and grimy from what could have only been a fall off the dreadful horse he'd just purchased, they didn't bat an eye. They shook his hand and watched as Julia accepted the dirty hug in kind. Each brother doted upon her. Flowers, kisses to the cheek, a fresh glass of wine. So far, they'd made her feel like a princess, and he hoped it would forever be that way. Alice washed her hands at the sink and accepted the towel Annie offered before popping it against Graham's leg. He jumped as she winked on her way towards the table.

"Clint, get those steaks going. We're all hungry." Annie swatted Julia out of the kitchen and towards the dining table. "We've got this, Julia. Lord knows you will be in here more than anybody now that you're back, so enjoy this small break while you can, honey. Hayes Matthew, don't you dare touch those carrot sticks until you show me proof you washed those hands."

Hayes froze, lifting his palms up as if he were a five-year-old caught with his hand in the cookie jar. Pam and Rodney chuckled at the fierce Annie and the way she bossed the boys around.

Graham fidgeted as Pam and Rodney bounced their gazes from one person to the next, from the floor of the room to the ceiling and every nook and cranny in between. They were giving his life a thorough comb through while they were here. He couldn't blame them. Their daughter was moving to a new state to be with a man they barely knew. He prayed he measured up and that they appreciated what they saw. He also hoped they enjoyed Annie's company and saw what an asset she was to his family and would be to Julia.

"Your house is lovely, Graham." Pam smiled in appreciation as Seth topped off her glass of sweet tea.

The screen door opened, and Philip walked inside. "About time you showed up." Lawrence rubbed his stomach. "I was already callin' dibs on your steak."

"You wish." Philip removed his hat and hung it on one of the many hooks above the doorway. His sight landed on Julia and he hugged her around the shoulders. "So, you really did come back."

"I did." She grinned as she snuggled closer into Graham's side. "These are my parents, Pam and Rodney." She motioned towards the nice couple as they eyeballed Philip in the measuring way they had all the others. "This is Philip," Julia explained. "He runs the feed store in town."

Nodding in welcome, Philip's stagnant stance was interrupted by Annie thrusting a bowl of salad in his hands for him to set on the table as he sat. He obeyed without a word.

Clint walked inside carrying a tray of steaks, the tantalizing smell encouraging everyone else in the kitchen and living room to all find their seats at the table. Graham appreciated his family coming together to make Julia's move to the 7H a special moment. He also appreciated her parents and the way his brothers made every attempt to be on their best behavior to make a good impression. For him. He knew they were trying to act their best so as not to scare Julia's parents. Seven grown men surrounding their only daughter could only be worrisome. And based on their smiles, he was pleased to see they were at ease around his family. It was obvious Julia was loved by all. He felt her slide her hand in his and bow her head.

Clearing his throat, he struggled with the words to say. He'd never felt so happy, so content, so overwhelmed with gratitude. At his silence, he felt Calvin slap a hand on his back and squeeze behind his neck as his brother said a prayer of thanks for the meal and for Julia and her family. Grateful, Graham nodded his thanks after the amen.

"You okay?" Julia whispered, leaning towards him, her hair swinging down over her shoulder. He nodded as he gently tucked it behind her and forced a smile. "You sure?"

"Just... thankful."

Her eyes, moistened by sudden restrained tears, glittered at him as she softly kissed his lips. "Me too, Graham. Me too."

KATHARINE E. HAMILTON

Continue the story with

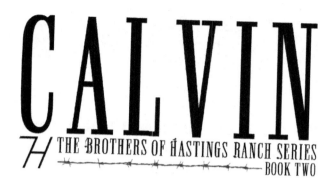

Order Here:
https://www.amazon.com/dp/B087N9DL7T

INTRODUCING THE FAMILY O'Rifcan

THE SIBLINGS O'RIFCAN SERIES KATHARINE E. HAMILTON

The Complete Siblings O'Rifcan Series Available in Paperback, Ebook, and Audiobook

Claron

https://www.amazon.com/dp/B07FYR44KX

Riley

https://www.amazon.com/dp/B07G2RBD8D

Layla

https://www.amazon.com/dp/B07HJRL67M

Chloe

https://www.amazon.com/dp/B07KB3HG6B

Murphy

https://www.amazon.com/dp/B07N4FCY8V

**All titles in The Lighthearted Collection
Available in Paperback, Ebook, and
Audiobook**

Chicago's Best

https://www.amazon.com/dp/B06XH7Y3MF

Montgomery House

https://www.amazon.com/dp/B073T1SVCN

Beautiful Fury

https://www.amazon.com/dp/B07B527N57

**Check out the Epic Fantasy Adventure
Available in Paperback, Ebook, and
Audiobook**

The Unfading Lands

The Unfading Lands
https://www.amazon.com/dp/B00VKWKPES

**Darkness Divided, Part Two in
The Unfading Lands Series**
https://www.amazon.com/dp/B015QFTAXG

**Redemption Rising, Part Three in
The Unfading Lands Series**
https://www.amazon.com/dp/B01G5NYSEO

Subscribe to Katharine's Newsletter for news on upcoming releases and events!
https://www.katharinehamilton.com/subscribe.html

Find out more about Katharine and her works at:
www.katharinehamilton.com

Social Media is a great way to connect with Katharine. Check her out on the following:

Facebook: Katharine E. Hamilton
https://www.facebook.com/Katharine-E-Hamilton-282475125097433/

Twitter: @AuthorKatharine
Instagram: @AuthorKatharine

Contact Katharine:
khamiltonauthor@gmail.com

ABOUT THE AUTHOR

Katharine E. Hamilton began writing in 2008 and published her first children's book, The Adventurous Life of Laura Bell in 2009. She would go on to write and illustrate two more children's books, Susie At Your Service and Sissy and Kat between 2010-2013.

Though writing for children was fun, Katharine moved into Adult Fiction in 2015 with her release of The Unfading Lands, a clean, epic fantasy that landed in Amazon's Hot 100 New Releases on its fourth day of publication, reached #72 in the Top 100 in Epic Fantasy, and hit the Top 10,000 Best Sellers on all of Amazon in its first week. It has been listed as a Top 100 Indie Read for 2015 and a nominee for a Best Indie Book Award for 2016. The series did not stop there. Darkness Divided: Part Two of The Unfading Land Series, released in October of 2015 and claimed a spot in the Top 100 of its genre. Redemption Rising: Part Three of The Unfading Lands Series released in April 2016 and claimed a nomination for the Summer Indie Book Awards.

Though comfortable in the fantasy genre, Katharine decided to venture towards romance in 2017 and released the first novel in a collection of sweet, clean and wholesome romances: The Lighthearted Collection. Chicago's Best reached best seller status in its first week of publication and rested comfortably in the Top 100 for Amazon for three steady weeks, claimed a Reader's Choice Award, a TopShelf Indie Book Award, and ended up a finalist in the American Book Festival's

Best Book Awards for 2017. Montgomery House, the second in the collection, released in August of 2017 and rested comfortably alongside its predecessor, claiming a Reader's Choice Award, and becoming Katharine's best-selling novel up to that point. Both were released in audiobook format in late 2017 and early 2018. Beautiful Fury is the third novel released in the collection and has claimed a Reader's Choice Award and a gold medal in the Authorsdb Best Cover competition. It has also been released in audiobook format with narrator Chelsea Carpenter lending her talents to bring it to life. Katharine and Chelsea have partnered on an ongoing project for creating audiobook marketing methods for fellow authors and narrators, all of which will eventually be published as a resource tool for others.

In August of 2018, Katharine brought to life a new clean contemporary romance series of a loving family based in Ireland. The Siblings O'Rifcan Series kicked off in August with Claron. Claron climbed to the Top 1000 of the entire Amazon store and has reached the Top 100 of the Clean and Wholesome genre a total of 11 times. He is Katharine's bestselling book thus far and lends to the success of the following books in the series: Riley, Layla, Chloe, and Murphy, each book earning their place in the Top 100 of their genre and Hot 100 New Releases. Claron was featured in Amazon's Prime Reading program March – June 2019. The series is also available in audiobook format with the voice talents of Alex Black.

A Love For All Seasons, a Sweet Contemporary Romance Series launched in July of 2019 with

Summer's Catch, followed by Autumn's Fall in October. Winter's Call and Spring's Hope scheduled for 2021 release dates. The series follows a wonderful group of friends from Friday Harbor, Washington, and has been Katharine's newest and latest project.

Katharine has contributed to charitable Indie Anthologies as well as helped other aspiring writers journey their way through the publication process. She manages an online training course that walks fellow self-publishing and independently publishing writers through the publishing process as well as how to market their books.

She is a member of Women Fiction Writers of America, Texas Authors, IASD, and the American Christian Fiction Writers. She loves everything to do with writing and loves that she is able to continue sharing heartwarming stories to a wide array of readers.

Katharine graduated from Texas A&M University with a bachelor's degree in History. She lives on a ranch in south Texas with her husband Brad, son Everett, another son on the way, West, and their two dogs, Tulip and Paws.